Vertue Rewarded;

OR, THE

IRISH Princess

Princess Grace Irish Library: 7

The Princess Grace Irish Library Series
(ISSN 0269-2619)
General Editor: C. George Sandulescu

1. ASSESSING THE 1984 *ULYSSES*.
   C. George Sandulescu and Clive Hart (editors)
2. IRISHNESS IN A CHANGING SOCIETY.
   The Princess Grace Irish Library (editor)
3. YEATS THE EUROPEAN. A. Norman Jeffares (editor)
4. *ULYSSES*: A REVIEW OF THREE TEXTS.
   Philip Gaskell and Clive Hart
5. THE LITERARY WORKS OF JACK B. YEATS.
   John W. Purser
6. THE CELTIC CONNECTION. Glanville Price (editor)
7. VERTUE REWARDED; OR, THE *IRISH* PRINCESS.
   Hubert McDermott (editor)

Vertue Rewarded;

OR, THE

IRISH Princess

Edited with an Introduction by
Hubert McDermott

Princess Grace Irish Library: 7

Originally Printed for *R Bentley*,
at the Post-house in Russel-street
in *Covent Garden*, London
1693

COLIN SMYTHE
Gerrards Cross, 1992

For Walter Allen

Introduction and Notes copyright © 1992
by Hubert McDermott

First Published in 1693
This edition first published in 1992 by
COLIN SMYTHE LIMITED
Gerrards Cross, Buckinghamshire
as the seventh volume in
The Princess Grace Irish Library Series

All Rights Reserved

Conditions of Sale
1. This book is sold subject to the condition that it shall not, by way of trade or otherwise, be lent, re-sold, hired out or otherwise circulated in any form of binding or cover other than that in which it is published and without a similar condition including this condition being imposed on the subsequent purchaser.
2. This book is sold subject to the Standard Conditions of Sale of Net Books and may not be re-sold in the UK below the net price fixed by the publishers for the book.

British Library Cataloguing in Publication Data
is available from the British Library

ISBN 0-86140-305-3 hb

Produced in Great Britain

INTRODUCTION[1]

VERTUE REWARDED; or, The Irish Princess, A New Novel, was published in London in 1693. An intriguing feature of the work is that its author is unknown. Even that indispensable guide to anonymous literature by Halkett and Laing[2] makes no mention of *Vertue Rewarded* never mind suggesting a possible author. This, however, is fairly easy to explain, since, in almost twenty years of research on early English fiction, I have seldom found reference to *Vertue Rewarded*. Indeed, it was while in search of another early work of fiction that I first discovered *Vertue Rewarded*. It had actually been bound in with several other fictional works by some enterprising publisher as a "special offer" compendium volume. The work was never reprinted.

The story of *Vertue Rewarded* is relatively simple to relate. In the year 1690, a prince serving in the army of King William of Orange is billeted in the town of Clonmel in Ireland. On his first day in the town the prince falls violently in love with a Clonmel girl. He is determined to have an affair with the girl and makes numerous attempts to seduce her. Finally, the girl's virtue is rewarded by the prince's agreeing to marry her, and she becomes an "Irish princess".

There is no great historical detail in *Vertue Rewarded*, but the little there is proves quite absorbing for an Irish reader. Volume four of E. A. D'Alton's *History of Ireland*[3] details the events of 1690. When William of Orange defeated King James at the battle of the Boyne in July 1690, the Irish army retreated first to Dublin and then to Limerick. William's transports were, in the meantime, in Dublin bay and in serious danger from a possible attack by the French. William, therefore, decided to secure Waterford as a safer place of refuge for his transports, and proceeded to march south with this in mind. It was this decision which took him to Clonmel, which he captured, before going on to take

v

Waterford. William then returned to Carrick-on-Suir where he left his army under the command of Count Solmes before he returned to Dublin. In August, he returned to his army and by August 9 was before the walls of Limerick ready to commence the famous siege. After much ado, however, William was forced to abandon the siege on August 30, and soon afterwards he went back to England.

In the novel we learn that King William "had then amongst his Forreign Troops several petty Princes who fought under him."(6) The hero of the novel is one of these petty princes, but his full name is never given in the novel: he is called the Prince of S——g, or 'Prince S——g'. The prince's principality is, we are informed, a small one, "not affording him an Income agreeable to his High Title"(6). The prince, therefore, resolved "to acquire that Plenty which his Fortune had denied him, and show by his Valour, that he was nothing beholding to her for giving him Titles, but rather that she was unkind, in not giving him as plentiful a revenue, as suited with the largeness of his Heart, and the vaster extent of his Merit. To this intent he came over the Sea in a small Command. . . ."(6) The presence of a foreign prince in William's army was by no means unique. D'Alton refers specifically to the presence of Prince George of Denmark, "several English nobles, some of them officers in his army, and some being volunteers."[4] One of William's senior commanders, Schomberg, was a Palatine duke. D'Alton continues: "The soldiers in William's army were of many nations, and had come from many lands: from England and from Scotland, and from the counties of Ulster, from the valleys of Switzerland . . . from the planes of Brandenberg, from France, from Sweden, and Norway, and Denmark. . . ."[5]

Vertue Rewarded describes the aftermath of the Battle of the Boynes as follows: "When our present King had fought the Battle at the *Boyne*, and drove the routed enemy into *Limerick*, he endeavoured to root up the War, by reducing that obstinate City, that durst hold out alone against the force of three Kingdoms, united in a Royal Army. . . ."(6) Eventually, King William arrives in Clonmel and the hero of *Vertue Rewarded* must accompany him to Limerick, leaving his loved one behind.

Introduction vii

When the prince arrives in Limerick, however, he writes love letters to his sweetheart in Clonmel in which he relates not only his great love for her, but also explains how the Williamite army is succeeding at the siege. "We have block'd your Enemies up", he writes, "won a Fort from them, and daily gain more ground. . . ."(78) D'Alton, in his commentary on the siege, remarks: "From the bastions and towers of the Irish town the guns inflicted loss on the Williamites, and from a battery across the river, in the English town, the advanced trenches were swept by an enfilading fire. Nevertheless, the besiegers made progress. They captured two redoubts, which the Irish held, though not without heavy loss; they advanced their trenches, and played at short range with their guns on the portion of the wall near St. John's gate, and with such effect that a breach of 36 feet wide was made; and on the 27th of August an attack in force was made."[6] D'Alton goes on to describe at length the attack on the Irish town and its consequences. Over 2,000 of the Williamite army were either killed or wounded, and it was this setback which finally decided William on abandoning his efforts to take Limerick. But the author of *Vertue Rewarded* tells a somewhat different version of events at Limerick: he has, for instance, the Williamites taking the Irish town (p. 80), and all set to take Limerick itself when disaster strikes them in the form of one Patrick Sarsfield. The author of *Vertue Rewarded* describes what happened.

". . . the Prince spake what he truly thought, that *Limerick* would soon be taken; for the king had sent for some heavy Cannon to the Camp, to throw down the walls, and a breach once made, there were thousands of *English* bold enough to have dared all the Enemies Shot, and force their way into the Town, in spite of all the resistance: but Fortune had otherwise ordered it, for Sarsfeild with an unusual Bravery, marched with a small body of Horse, farther into that part of the Country which was Subjected to the English Power than they suspected he durst; surprized the Convoy, and cutting them to pieces burnt them, their Carriages and Provisions, (which they brought for the Army) to ashes; some of the Carriages he nailed up and burst the rest; and the Army wanting them to batter the walls, and the hasty approach of the Winter, not giving them time to send for others, they raised the Siege; his Majesty went for *England*; his Forces retired to their Winter Quarters. . . ."(80)

The foregoing does not mean that the author of *Vertue Rewarded* was misinformed about events in Limerick in August 1690. Rather, what we have here is an excellent example of "faction", where the raising of the siege of Limerick by the extraordinary bravery of Sarsfield and his men is much more vivid and dramatic than what actually took place. In fact, the siege of Limerick commenced on 9 August, 1690, and the blowing up of the Williamite convoy at Ballyneety occurred on the following day, 10 August. William continued to besiege Limerick for a further three weeks.

The anonymous author of *Vertue Rewarded* shows himself quite familiar with Clonmel and its environs. At the start of the novel he describes Clonmel as "a City in the County of *Tipperary*, scituated in a large Plain near the Sewer [Suir], now grown obscure, formerly famous for the great Battel fought just by it, between two Brothers who were Competitors for the Crown of Mounster; when that famous Island had five Crowned Heads to Govern its Inhabitants".(7) A feature of Clonmel is that, when necessary, armies had to be billeted on the population, and this provides the basis of most of the action in *Vertue Rewarded* because the prince and the part of the Williamite army under his command foist themselves on the people of Clonmel. Later, when he is attempting to prosecute his affair with his loved one, Marinda, the prince continually visits the house where she lives, on the pretence of visiting the soldiers billeted there. Later, he actually billets himself in the same house as Marinda. In other respects, too, the anonymous author shows his familiarity with the town of Clonmel. Marinda, for instance lives in High Street in the town, a street which did, and still does, exist. This seemingly trivial fact becomes more impressive when one realises that the typical Irish town — unlike its English counterpart — seldom has a High Street. An old ruined Abbey also features in the novel, a minor Character, Celadon commencing an adventure there one night and waking up there at the end of the adventure, on a tombstone, with "no cloaths, but an old Franciscan habit"(25) on him. In fact, the Franciscan order came to Clonmel in 1269 and within a number of years had built the Abbey in question. This Abbey was taken from them in 1543, and sold for £48. In 1650 it was taken possession of by the Cromwellians who turned it into a temporary fortress. Thereafter, it fell into disrepair, and was, almost certainly, by 1690, as described in *Vertue Rewarded*. Finally, there is an interpolated story in *Vertue Rewarded* at the centre of which is a holy well located outside the town of Clonmel. In the main plot, the prince takes a nap beside this same holy well, and awakens to hear a vital conversation between Marinda and her confidante. Here, again, the anonymous author's familiarity with the town is demonstrated since the area does have a holy well, one of some repute even today.

A ball is held in Clonmel, early in the story at the house of "The Great Moracho". "Moracho", in spite of its seeming strangeness is in fact an anglicisation of "Murchú", or, more correctly, "Ó Murchú". When the author, therefore, talks of a ball at Moracho's he is in effect saying that a ball was held at "Murphy's" house, where "Murphy" is simply a sobriquet for the eminent local dignitary. Although it would be a significant coincidence if the dignitary's name in question was actually Moracho or its equivalent, it is worth noting that W. P. Burke in his *History of Clonmel*[7] gives a list of "old burghers" of the town who were, in 1661, recommended to the Duke of Ormond for "favourable consideration". Among the "old burghers" listed is a Willim Morroghow — an anglicisation of Murchú not far removed from Moracho.

It seems quite unlikely that the authorship of *Vertue Rewarded* will ever be discovered. One possibility is that the author was an Englishman serving in the Williamite army, thereby gaining first-hand knowledge of Clonmel as well as of military and political developments in Ireland. It is more likely, however, that the writer was someone of planter stock in Ireland — perhaps also involved with the Williamites, though not necessarily so. For a better understanding of *Vertue Rewarded* it is important that the twentieth-century reader understand what is meant by the phrase "planter stock". In the latter half of the seventeenth century there were, in Ireland, two distinct communities.[8] One of these was a planter community, people mostly of English, Welsh and Scottish stock who had settled in Ireland as planters in the latter half of the sixteenth and the early part of the seventeenth century. These settlers regarded themselves as anything but Irish, since they despised the native Irish. Nevertheless, with the passing of time, events conspired to make these settlers realise that they were as distinct from the inhabitants of England, Scotland and Wales as they were from the native Irish. And by the early 1600s, the settlers had actually come to call themselves Irish.[9] No sooner had they adopted this new identity, however, than the rising of 1641 occurred, a rising which had as one of its aims the ridding of Ireland of all settlers. Almost inevitably the settlers rejected their newfound Irish identity and began to call themselves British Protestants. But *Vertue Rewarded* shows, significantly, that by 1693 the settlers had one again reverted to the description "Irish". Marinda is, therefore, a daughter of a protestant settler in Ireland, so that William is her king and Sarsfield and company are regarded as the enemies of her "Liberty and Religion"(7).

The "second community", i.e., the native Irish, deserve some mention, too, in particular the attitudes of the English towards them. Edmund Spenser's *A View of the Present State of Ireland*, written in 1596, synopsises English attitudes to the native Irish which had been prevalent from the early years of the thirteenth century. Spenser argues, like numerous writers before him, that the genealogical stemma of the native Irish could be traced to the most barbaric people known to Western man — the Scythians. This barbaric people was particularly associated with sheep herding. The native Irish were, therefore, regarded by the English and the settlers as very much like their progenitors, the Scythians — degenerate, debased, uncivilised. In numerous historical documents, over hundreds of years, one recurring epithet which seems to sum up English and settler attitudes towards the native Irish is "wild" — the wild Irish.

In *Vertue Rewarded*, by implication at least, attitudes have not changed. The first native Irishman to feature in the work, though only incidentally, is the Great Moracho who is described as being "famous all over the Kingdom for his Riches, particularly in his flocks of Sheep, as numerous as those of the mighty Scythian. . . ."(10) Later in the book a girl describes six suitors she has rejected. Number seven is different, however: "When he paid a visit, if any of the rest of the suitors chanced to come at the same time, the Breeding which he brought from *Dublin*, elevated him so far above them, in his Discourse, his Carriage, and all he did, that they did look like our Wild *Irish* to him. . . ."(20): This comment, as well as casting the conventional slur on the native Irish and their degeneracy, also highlights the narrow scope of *Vertue Rewarded*. The work was almost certainly written by a member of the Irish planter community *about* that community. And *Vertue Rewarded* could also be regarded as a propaganda work on behalf of the Irish planter community, emphasising as it does the sophistication, good breeding and excellent education of the heroine, Marinda — qualities which are no less than one would expect to find in one actually born and reared a princess.

Vertue Rewarded; or, the Irish Princess, A New Novel is a work which had been almost totally neglected since its publication almost two hundred years ago.[10] In compensation for three centuries of obscurity, however, *Vertue Rewarded* could yet find itself one of the most significant works in the canon of pre-Richardson fiction. To understand why this might be, it is necessary to offer a brief survey of some developments in fiction in the seventeenth and eighteenth centuries.

The significant occurrence in fiction in seventeenth-century Europe was the rise of the heroic romance in France. This type of fiction was basically derived from ancient Greek romance and the plot is essentially the same in each. In the French romance a boy and girl fall madly in love with each other at first sight, and the story goes on to detail their numerous adventures from the time they meet until their eventual marriage. The couple are usually prevented from marrying earlier by one or several reasons: parental opposition, disparity in rank, the threat of incest, machinations of villains, and intrigues of rivals. Eventually, all difficulties are resolved, sometimes miraculously, and the boy and girl can marry. A significant feature of heroic romance is the unqualified acceptance by all heroes and heroines that no matter how passionate or overwhelming their love, it is subject to the higher demands of duty — duty to one's parents in particular, but also to one's country. Indeed, duty is of such importance in the heroic romances that each one could be aptly subtitled *Love and Duty Reconciled*, since this is the only way in which a happy ending can be brought about. If the heroine's father objects to her lover, or if the hero is an enemy of her country, she knows and accepts that there is only one course open to her, the dutiful one. Luckily, the Gordian knot is invariably cut, and love and duty are finally reconciled. Another feature of the heroic romance is the propensity for each and every minor character to tell his or her own story: on occasions, these interpolated stories run to an even greater length than the main one. For this and other reasons, the heroic romances were known as "*romans a longue haleine*" — "longwinded romances". The best known of the romances were Gomberville's *Polexandre* (1632) and *Citherée* (1640-'42); the Scudérys' *Ibrahim* (1641), *Artamene* (1649) and *Clélie* (1656); and Calprenède's *Cassandra* (1642), *Cleopatra* (1648), and *Pharamond* (1662).

The history of fiction in England during the first half of the seventeenth century presents a picture totally different to that in France: it was, in effect, almost totally moribund. The resuscitation came from France, where, as early as 1625, forces had been at work preparing the way for the reception of the French heroic romance. In that year Charles I had married a sixteen-year-old French princess named Henrietta Maria. Soon afterwards a strong current of French influence passed into England, affecting — at first at any rate — the circle of society surrounding the royal court. Soon there were fervid English students of the sacred French texts of heroic romance, who read them, as E. A. Baker remarks: "Not only for amusement but also for edification, and trained themselves to think and feel and speak and behave according to the best French standards of breeding."[11] During the exile of the English court in France, the writing of heroic romance was at its height. Nor did the absence of the court from England affect the vogue of the romances there — the royalist families regarded the French romances as repositories of aristocratic values. One of the last acts of the King, Charles I, before he was executed, was to present the Earl of Lindsey with a copy of *Cassandra*, Calprenède's heroic romance. The heroic romances were read in England first in the original French by people who flaunted their ability to read and speak French fluently. The English translations of the French workers came much later: *Ibrahim* and *Cassandra* were translated in 1652, *Le Grand Cyrus* in 1653, *Cleopatra* in 1654, *Clelia* in 1659 and *Pharamond* in 1662. Soon the inevitable imitations began to appear, the first in 1653 by "a person of honour" and entitled *Cloria and Narcissus, or The Royal Romance*. Others to appear were *Panthalia* (1659), *Aretina* (1660), *Birinthia* (1664), and *Pandion and Amphigenia* (1665).

As the seventeenth century drew to a close, the vogue for heroic romance diminished greatly in England. Ioan Williams argues[12] that this diminution was a typical English rejection of the neoclassicism upon which the French had founded their prose fiction. But there were less academic, perhaps more important, forces at work, too, which affected the reception of the heroic romance in England. The most decisive of these forces was, perhaps, the return of the new, prosperous middle classes to the arts — both fiction and drama. The effect was soon felt in fiction. The chapbooks and indeed the vast majority of popular fiction with the exception of works such as *Pilgrim's Progress* was not to the liking of the new readers, and neither, as might well be imagined, was the heroic romance. The rise of the middle classes coincided with — could itself be said to have brought about — the revolution in the writing and publication of fiction. The patronage system had all but collapsed, and authors began to depend on the public for their livelihood: the bookseller/publisher became the middleman between the writer and public and saw to it that the middle classes were given what they wanted, or, at least initially, what he presumed they wanted. But the tastes of the aristocracy had changed, too, by the end of the century: they had become satiated with the bulk and complication of the heroic romance and were looking for something new. It can be said, therefore, with some qualification, that, at the end of the seventeenth century, the fictional tastes of both the middle and upper classes had coincided and that there was, at last, not two reading publics in England, but one.

The typical English reader considered the interminable length of heroic romance to be its major flaw. Mrs. Mary de La Riviere Manley, one of the female writers of fiction in the eighteenth century, believed the English had "naturally no Taste for long-winded Performances, for they have no longer sooner begun a Book but they desire to see an End of it. . . ."[13] The objections to length were easily overcome and there followed a somewhat abrupt shortening of prose fiction. Publishers sought a new name for the new short works, with the aim of distinguishing between them and the long romances. The term chosen was "novel", which thus adopted the connotation of a short romance. Mrs. Manley, for instance, talks of "These Little Pieces", as opposed to the "Prodigious length of the . . . Romances."[14] "A Novel", the Earl of Chesterfield wrote to his son, "is a kind of abbreviation of Romance . . ."[15]; and George Canning wrote in *The Microcosm* that novel writing had "by some later authors been aptly enough styled the younger sister of Romance. A family likeness indeed is very evident; and in their leading features, though in the one a more enlarged and in the other on a more contracted scale, a strong resemblance is easily discoverable between them."[16]

By the early years of the eighteenth century, a sufficient number of short works of prose fiction which were broadly similar in kind had been written so as to justify a new "label", and they are now generally known as "romances of passion" or "amorous novellas". These romances of passion were simply modifications of the situations, themes and style of heroic romances. Not that this modification was an improvement; it was, rather, what John Richetti calls "A simplification or vulgarisation"[17] of the heroic romance. Richetti goes on to claim that the "great majority of the amorous novellas written in English before 1740 merely condensed the excesses of the heroic romance, substituted a debased and inflated but simplified heroic rant for the involved *preciosité* of the romances, and used that style to deliver stories of some external complication but of extreme moral and emotional simplicity."[18] In a typical amorous novella/passionate romance, the heroine is usually beautiful, innocent, and defenceless; defenceless, that is, because she has no one to "protect" her: she is usually either an orphan or has only one parent living, almost invariably the mother. The typical hero of the passionate romance is usually an aristocratic libertine-seducer. He is captivated by the beauty of the heroine and sets out to possess her at any cost but marriage. A great deal of the story is taken up with his stratagems to rape or seduce the heroine: the ultimate stratagem is often a bogus marriage. The heroine, for her part, becomes a persecuted innocent, a persecution complicated by her having fallen in love with the rake. After very many "warm" or passionate scenes, the rake eventually enjoys the female through rape or seduction: the moment this is accomplished, he loses interest in the girl whom he then "abandons". She suffers one misfortune after another and becomes, at last, painfully aware of her folly. Her endless self-recriminations serve, supposedly, as a warning to other young women, but are, basically, an attempt to justify whatever lubricity might have appeared in the work. A feature of the romance of passion is that it continues the love-versus-duty conflict of the heroic romance, but with an interesting variation on the concept of duty. Duty in the heroic romance meant, as we saw, duty to one's parents or country: in the romance of passion, the duty of the heroine to her virtue and its preservation becomes paramount. Inevitably, this new conflict is a much more intense one, involving the heroine in a clash, not, as previously, with extraneous forces: henceforth the clash is between powerful forces within herself. The dilemma of the heroine is obvious: her passionate love for the male demands that she fulfil her love by giving herself to him, while her duty to her virtue demands that she refrain from doing so. The hero, too, has his own conflict between love and duty to contend with. His duty is to what is called his "interest", a word which occurs with great regularity in the romances of passion. Love and interest are, the hero invariably believes, incompatible. Love and duty are almost never reconciled in the romance of passion: love overcomes duty in the case of the female and *vice versa* in the case of the male. The love of the female is usually portrayed as an overwhelming passion which cannot be contained, with disastrous consequences for her. Neither, of course, can the passion of the male be contained: but his desires are sated without any sacrifice of duty, and without any ill consequences for him.

It is, perhaps, appropriate at this point to offer some explanation for the emergence of lubricity as a major ingredient in English fiction in the early eighteenth century. Licentiousness and indecency in fiction had been fostered as early as 1660 by the French *chroniques scandaleuses*, short, lurid accounts of illicit love affairs and other indiscretions amongst the nobility of the day. The popularity of these reports was as great in England as it was in France, and English imitators soon flourished, Mrs Behn being one of the first. It soon became apparent to the professional writers of fiction and their publishers that lubricity in fiction would be a much better seller than chastity, and they quickly made the necessary adjustments. Concomitantly, they devised a justification for lubricity, claiming an ulterior moral purpose for gross licentiousness. Passionate romance became one of the fictional vehicles in the early eighteenth century for the dissemination of this licentiousness.

The popularity of early eighteenth-century fiction was owing to more than a mere portrayal of lubricity, however. It was also a "fantasy machine" which presented an opportunity for the middle and lower classes to "participate vicariously in an erotically exciting and glittering fantasy world"[19] of the aristocracy. The romances of passion also reflected the "well-known eighteenth-century preoccupation"[20] with the myth of the destruction of female innocence, by representatives of the aristocratic world of male corruption. Richetti shows how the romances of passion "In spite of their stylized and extravagant characters and situations are firmly rooted in certain basic if distorted economic realities . . . the persecuted maiden's story is an oblique comment on the absolute economic dependence of eighteenth-century woman."[21]

By common consent, one of the earliest and best of the romances of the eighteenth century was *Lindamira*, published in 1702. Chronologically and otherwise *Lindamira* is generally viewed as a "half-way house" between the heroic romance of the seventeenth century and the realistic novel of the eighteenth. Benjamin Boyce, a modern editor of *Lindamira*, declares that one would be disinclined to believe that the "foreign art" of Madeleine de Scudery had fostered the fiction of Defoe, Richardson, and Fielding without *Lindamira* "To show how the thing could happen."[22] Boyce claims, too, that *Lindamira* is a "remarkable demonstration of how something of situation, motivation and sentiment could be abstracted from the rather *démodé* French heroic romance and adapted to English middle-class life".[23] The story tells, in epistolary form, of the love of Lindamira and Cleomidon and of the numerous obstacles which prevent their marrying, just as in the typical French romance. The major obstacle is an economic one: Cleomidon is not very well off, and his rich uncle will only settle his vast estate on him if he marries the wealthy Cleodora. Lindamira refuses to marry her lover, and thus deprive him of his fortune, so Cleomidon has little option but to marry Cleodora. Lindamira and Cleomidon are, however, rescued from their abject misery, years later, when Cleodora dies in childbirth. But other, typical difficulties arise and have also to be overcome before the lovers can finally marry.

John Richetti shares Boyce's enthusiasm for *Lindamira*: problems begin to arise, however, when he describes it as a "conventional if clearly rendered amatory novella."[24] An amatory novella *Lindamira* clearly is, but Richetti would obviously need to redefine his terms in order to describe this work as a typical eighteenth-century amatory novella. Richetti goes on to implicitly question the role of *Lindamira* as a model for later writers. The "rarity of performances such as *Lindamira*" he argues "must make us wonder why adaption of the heroic romance was not done more often."[25] He even has reservations about the characters in *Lindamira* vis-à-vis those of the typical romance of passion, and remarks, for instance, that Cleomidon's "good sense and decent reticence separate him at once from the equally gifted but emotionally compulsive heroes of the amatory novella I will discuss later."[26] Even Lindamira herself, Richetti admits, "is something of a rationalist who despises the cant phrases of love and its power."[27] Richetti's parting comments on *Lindamira* deserve quoting in order to show how he imagined later amatory novellas evolving from the 1702 work:

> The fable of virtue and constancy rewarded is promised and delivered in *Lindamira*, decently and reasonably dressed but present . . . in unmistakable terms. It may be that these ideological simplicities, only occasionally and unobtrusively visible in *Lindamira*, had as much to do with its modest success as the wit and realism we admire in it. That is debatable. What is certain is that these simplicities, further simplified and rendered in bright and lascivious colours, are the main features of the really popular amatory novella. Furthermore, it is this lurid paradigm, with its rich opportunities for pathetic and erotic involvement, that is of interest in the study of the pre-Richardson eighteenth-century novel; for it is within this popular tradition that the heroines of Richardson and Fielding are to make their tragic and comic points.[28]

Richetti's arguments here are of the *post hoc propter hoc* kind, since there would appear to be no discernible relationship between *Lindamira* and the typical amatory novel of the eighteenth century. The evolution which Richetti talks of — "simplicities further simplified and rendered in bright lascivious colours" — is nothing short of revolutionary. His unease is also revealed when he writes of the difference between Lindamira and "the *really popular* [my italics] amatory novella." The difficulty of critics is, of course, easy to understand: *Lindamira* is a work of some distinction, and it was, additionally, published sufficiently early to make it an obvious choice for those seeking prototypes for later development. But this, I think, is a line of argument no longer sustainable, if only because an earlier work exists which has a great deal more in common with the amatory novella of the eighteenth century than can be claimed for *Lindamira*; the work in question is, of course, *Vertue Rewarded*.

Vertue Rewarded follows the general pattern of a typical romance of passion. The heroine is a ravishing beauty, and she

Introduction

is also innocent and defenceless, with only another female, her mother, to protext her. The male is an aristocrat — a prince in this case — who is a typical libertine-seducer. One notable exception in this regard is that he has no "history" as later rakes do, that is, we are not explicitly told of any earlier conquests and "abandonments" of females by the prince. But in almost all other respects he is the typical rake of later fiction. Immediately on meeting and falling in love with Marinda, he is "resolved to enjoy her"(16). To enjoy her in marriage is, typically, out of the question, however. When his attempted seduction of Marinda is not progressing satisfactorily, the prince seeks help from a fortune-teller. One of her first queries is whether he intends marrying his loved one, and the prince replies as follows:

> Marriage! (Said the Prince) why did not I confess to you tht she was a private Gentlewoman, one beneath me? I wonder you should ask such a question.... If... I can enjoy her on any terms but those of Marriage, I shall think myself very happy; if not, my Love has so wholly blinded me as to make me forget my Interest and My Honour. (66)

Prince S——g is one of the earliest, if not the first of a long line of libertine-seducers from the pages of passionate romance. But in Marinda he meets, in effect, one of the last of the heroines from the pages of heroic romance. Marinda is, however, well aware that times have changed and there are no longer "heroic" males — or at least very few — in existence. Diana, a friend of Marinda, knowing that she had fallen violently in love with the prince, warns her of continued association with him, as follows:

> Have a care *Marinda* . . . that you do not engage too far with one who is so much above you: 'tis not safe Intriguing with Persons of his Quality; Inferiour Lovers may be jested with as long as we please, and thrown off at will, but such as he seldom leave us without carrying away our Vertue, or at least our Reputation: and you will too late curse your own Charms when they have exposed you to be ruined (like young Conjurers) by raising a Spirit which you are not able to lay. (33)

In her reply, Marinda shows herself to be a typical heroine from heroic romance:

I fear . . . S——g has spy'd something in my behaviour that (he fancied) favoured him, as Men conceitedness makes them apt to discover such things; I am sorry for it if I did discover any weakness in my self, that should encourage him to such an attempt: I am sure my Tongue never dropt the least word in his favour; and if my telltale Eyes, or my Countenance has betray'd me, I'll disfigure this Countenance, and tear out these Eyes, rather than they shall invite, or assist any enterprise, to the prejudice of my Vertue. (33)

In his pursuit of Marinda, the prince devises several stratagems to entrap her. The first is a ball which he secretly organizes and from which he pretends he will be absent. Three other stratagems depend on the circumstances in the town of Clonmel, viz., that the Williamite army is billeted on the population, including Marinda's mother. In order to gain access to his loved one, the prince continually pretends to visit the officers billeted in her house. Later, he pretends to have a falling out with the "Gentleman of His Horse" and good friend, Celadon. Celadon then leaves the prince's quarters where he has been staying, and foists himself on Marinda's mother as a lodger. Under the pretence of visiting his friend, Celadon, prince S——g gains constant access to Marinda. Finally, the prince actually billets himself in Marinda's house. Two other stratagems involve Celadon acting as the prince's agent. The prince's final attempt on Marinda's virtue involves a stratagem which crops up with monotonous regularity in later passionate romances, that is, the hero's inability to marry the heroine because he is already married. The typical heroine, on discovering that she can never have the hero "honourably", invariably falls into the trap set for her and allows herself to be seduced by the male. In *Vertue Rewarded* Celadon tells Marinda (via her friend, Diana), that the prince would marry her if he were not already married. Marinda's reaction to the news is a strictly virtuous one, however — she simply plans to leave the prince forever and is actually on her way out of the locality when attacked by bandits and forced to return home.

Vertue Rewarded continues, as might be expected, the heroic romance tradition of conflict between love and duty. Given the changed circumstances of the passionate romance, however, the conflict takes the new form described above. In *Vertue Rewarded*, the conflict is between Marinda's passionate love for the prince and her duty to her virtue. Although the conflict is intense, Marinda is always steadfast in her devotion to duty rather than to love. The refrain throughout, *Vertue Rewarded* is "my Innocence . . . which is dearer to me than Life . . . I must not sacrifice" (89). For the heroine, love and duty can only be reconciled by marriage, and this she eventually secures. The conflict between love and duty in the breast of the hero is also a new one, and in this case, too, it was to become typical of later conflicts in the passionate romances. This conflict is the one between the hero's love for the heroine and his so-called duty to his interest or ambition, based on the disparity of rank between him and the girl. In *Vertue Rewarded*, as we have already seen above, the prince cannot even visualize the possibility of marriage to one "beneath" him, and states that love has not so blinded him as to make him forget his "Interest and his . . . Honour" (66). In the typical, later romance of passion, interest or ambition usually wins out, but in *Vertue Rewarded* the prince's love for Marinda overcomes his concern for his interest and his honour, and he marries her.

Inevitably, because it is such an early romance of passion, *Vertue Rewarded* differs in some respects from later models. Some of these distinctions have already been implied — for instance *Vertue Rewarded* ends in marriage, an event which was to be exceptional in later versions. In addition, while there is a great deal of "passion" both implied and stated explicitly in *Vertue Rewarded*, there are no scenes which could be described as "warm" and there is no lubricity as such. Indeed, whenever the author of *Vertue Rewarded* finds himself confronted with a scene which offers possibilities for a "warm" description he tends to back off. The author even claims at one point that he has good reason for not explicitly describing the lover's passions: "neither would he [the author] think it safe to express them to the Life if he could, lest a Passion so well represented might prove infectious to those that Read it; and such Charming Words like those in magical Books, might raise a Spirit in some Fair Reader's Mind, some rampant Spirit, that would make the Raiser his prey, before she would be able to lay him again" (81). The implications of these remarks are obvious: and equally obvious are the possibilities for developing such scenes as are passed over in *Vertue Rewarded*. And yet, in spite of all that has been said, *Vertue Rewarded* does have one scene which might qualify as a "warm" one. In this scene, Marinda is telling her friend Diana of her passionate love for the prince. She then goes on to describe a dream she has had:

... as the thoughts of the day have an effect upon those at night, I believe these were the cause of my being disturbed in my Bed with this Dream. The Prince, methought, in my absence, had hidden himself in my Bed-chamber, and, when I came in, started out upon me: He had on one side of him a little wing'd Archer, who bent his Bow, and aimed at me several times; but just by me there started up a great Gigantick form, with no other Arms but a Shield, and he, methought, still interposed that, and with it kept off the Arrows of the other; at length, methought, the Prince spoke something which tempted my Defender over to his side, and left me to the Mercy of the young Archer, who shot me through and through and at the same instant the Prince came and catch'd me in his Arms, and told me I was his Prisoner, at which I swooned away with a pleasing pain, and at the fright of it I awaked. (32)

It is relatively obvious that not only is there a substantial difference between *Vertue Rewarded* and *Lindamira*, but also that *Vertue Rewarded* can be seen as a prototype for later developments in English passionate romance. Perhaps the best way to demonstrate the relationship between the 1693 work and later romances of passion, is to choose one for purposes of comparison.

The passionate romance I have chosen to discuss is one written by Mrs Mary de la Riviere Manley in 1720, and entitled "The Wife's Resentment". This work is the third of seven published under the title *The Power of Love* in 1720. Mrs Manley was one of the most prolific of the so-called "women scribblers" of the early years of the eighteenth century, and also one of the most influential. She was particularly known for her expertise in "warm" scenes. The story of "The Wife's Resentment" is relatively simple to relate. The work is set in Spain, where the hero, Count Roderigo Ventimiglia, falls passionately in love at first sight with a beautiful girl of low degree called Violenta. The count pursues Violenta relentlessly over a period of eighteen months before rewarding her virtue by making her a countess. But the story does not end there: Count Roderigo contracts a second, bigamous marriage to a woman of his own class, and abandons Violenta who lives up to her name by killing him violently.

The count and Violenta meet in much the same way as do the prince and Marinda in *Vertue Rewarded*. In *Vertue Rewarded*, the prince is riding down the main street in Clonmel, when he spies Marinda at a window: her beauty "Fixed his sight", we are told, "as if she alone were worthy of his Attention: He continued looking that way, and turned not his Eyes off the Window, till the fieryness of his Horse . . . had carried him beyond the House . . ." (7). Likewise, in "The Wife's Resentment", Count Roderigo is passing by Violenta's house when he sees her at the door. he is "disarmed by the Flashes of her Eyes", and "staid some times to gaze on her that had wounded him to so dangerous a degree".[29] Both heroes and heroines fall in love at first sight.

Like Marinda, Violenta is "a poor orphan kept by her Mother who had been some Years a Widow" (180). Unlike Marinda, however, Violenta does not appear defenceless, since she has two older brothers who are prosperous jewellers. In fact, however, when Violenta is dishonoured, she discovers that "their Souls were of a Piece with their Profession, they did not dream of Honour and Revenge provided they could sell their Plate" (203). For both heroines, loss of virtue is synonymous with loss of life. Marinda writes to the prince saying that her innocence "which is dearer to me than . . . Life . . . I must not sacrifice, no, not to you" (89). And it is in a letter, too, that Violenta states her case to the count. She says she is "a Maid . . . who knows the true estimation of Vertue, and would die in the Defence of it" (182). Later, Marinda accuses the prince of defending her virtue from others in order to "Prey upon it your self" (84), and Violenta accuses the count of being a "Persecutor of Vertue . . . a Tyrant that would force from me the only Treasure I possess!" (191). In each work, the heroine continues to have a great deal to say on the subject of virtue. Each continually threatens to put her virtue beyond the reach of her attacker, yet, each seems so spellbound by the male as to be incapable of acting on her threats. Marinda, when she hears that the prince is married, does attempt to run away, but when the attempt is accidentally foiled, does not persevere in her intention. The virtue of both Marinda and Violenta is "rewarded' by marriage to a nobleman. Count Roderigo sees himself as one who will "reward her Chastity" (190), by marrying Violenta, while the author of *Vertue Rewarded* tells us that "the beautiful *Marinda* received the reward of her invincible Vertue . . ." (103).

Count Roderigo and Prince S——g are two typical aristocratic libertine-seducers and both use agents, initially, to discover particulars of their loved ones. What strikes both the count and the prince is the effect that this particular woman above all others has had on him. The prince remarks on all the "excellent beauties" (14), he has seen and "How indifferent I was to them all" (15). For the count also, "this was the first time his [heart] was ever touch'd (182): previously "all Women were equally indifferent to him, he had no more Esteem or Tenderness for one than another. . ." (176). Each of the heroes is taken by the wit as well as the beauty of his beloved, and each sets out to seduce her as quickly as possible. Both the count and the prince go on to devise stratagems to overcome the virtue of his particular sweetheart. We have already looked at the stratagems employed by the prince, and those of the count are not dissimilar. The count specializes, however, in financial stratagems — using his vast wealth in attempts to "buy" the virtue of Violenta. When he fails to make an impression on Violenta herself, he offers her mother one thousand gold ducats as an incentive to procure a husband for her daughter — "provided she would have some small Considerations of his [Count Roderigo's] Suffering and afford him a little Ease from that intolerable Rack he endur'd!" (188). Violenta's mother replies, saying her house is "no place to purchase virtue in" (189), and quickly sends him packing. Roderigo also uses his wealth in another attempt on the virtue of Violenta. He discovers that Violenta intends to visit a friend of hers, and "by the Force of Presents, got leave of that Person to conceal himself in her Closet till *Violenta* came. . ." (184). When Violenta arrives, Roderigo starts out upon her, but achieves nothing.

The prince and the count eventually find themselves in identical predicaments, and they express their frustration in quite similar terms. The prince tells the fortune-teller that his love "is one so violent and yet so unreasonable, that I am unable to curb it, nor have I any hopes of success if I let it go on" (64). Count Roderigo, for his part, discovers that he cannot "abandon the Maid, That he had in vain essay'd; he could not by Diversion drive her out of his Thoughts, That was a fruitless Project; he could not corrupt her, nor could he not live without her!" (189). Both heroes claim that they will die if their sweethearts will not facilitate them. The prince pleads with Marinda ". . . do not rashly resolve on my Ruin, but consider . . . whether it is not juster for your Pity to indulge that Passion, which your Disdain cannot destroy: and so instead of proving the Death of your Lover give him his Life. . ." (78). For his part, the Count says to Violenta: "I die for you, but you will not pity me!" (185). The prince and the count could easily alleviate their respective frustrations by simply marrying their loved ones: but such a possibility seems quite unimaginable to either male. When the fortune-teller inquires of the prince if he intends to marry Marinda, he thinks it sufficient to point that she "is a private Gentlewoman, one beneath me" (66). "I wonder you should ask such a question" (66), he adds. Additionally, this love-versus-duty conflict manifests itself in the continual self-recriminations which the prince indulges in. He talks of his "mean Passion" (67), for Marinda, and later, "Placed his . . . Folly in the first rank . . . to cringe to one that was beneath him, and to submit himself to one who could not pretend to a higher match than one of his Dependants. . ." (75). The count has similar problems which he expresses in a manner similar to the prince: "Yet, as much in Love as Roderigo was, during all that Time, he never once thought of marrying her: the Disparity between them was so great he had no Notion of Wedlock"(184). Later, we are told that despite the extremity of his love for Violenta, Roderigo cannot "bring himself . . . to debase his Blood so far as to mingle by

Marriage with one of her low Degree" (186), and he resolves to cure himself of "so infamous and uneasy a Passion" (186). Both men finally offer marriage to their respective sweethearts, but, given their previous strong, seemingly unyielding, opposition to marriage, both have to make certain psychological adjustments. And the adjustment in both "*Vertue Rewarded* and "The Wife's Resentment" is almost identical: each hero arrives at the conclusion that he could not, after all, have married a better woman. The count, for instance, eventually forms the opinion that though Violenta "was neither of such Birth or Fortune as his Quality deserv'd, yet her Vertue and Accomplishments, her Beauty and Discretion deserv'd greater Advancement!" (189). And he later tells Violenta that he has "no less a Value" for her than if she "were descended from the noblest Family in Spain" (196). In *Vertue Rewarded*, the prince, too, reassures himself as follows: "You deserve all things Divine *Marinda* . . . what Title is too High or Estate too Magnificent to admit you for a Partner? I will no more indulge this vain Ambition or let it cross my Love: tell me *Celadon*, (*said he*) does not *Marinda*, with her natural Beauty look finer than our Proudest Court Ladies, tho' decked with all their Gaudy Costly Dresses? Yet that lovely Body is but the shell of a more glorious Inhabitant . . ." (90).

Apart from other, minor similarities between *Vertue Rewarded* and "The Wife's Resentment", one is particularly struck by the occurrence of a dream in each work, and in each the future predicted in the dream comes true. In *Vertue Rewarded*, Marinda's dream foretells her sexual surrender to Prince S——g (though it does not reveal whether this surrender will be within the bounds of marriage or otherwise). And in 'The Wife's Resentment", Count Roderigo dreams of his own violent death at the hands of his wife — an event which comes to pass. One final aspect of *Vertue Rewarded* and "the Wife's Resentment" which is worth remarking, is that there is no strictly "warm" scene in either work. Such an omission seems particularly exceptional for a work written in 1720 by the acknowledged expert in such scenes — Mrs Manley: but she does, at least, confirm her reputation in the remainder of *The Power of Love*.

Introduction

The basic difference between *Vertue Rewarded* and "The Wife's Resentment" is, perhaps, that the Manley work depicts a rake's progress prior to his meeting his loved one, and goes on depicting that progress after his marriage. *Vertue Rewarded*, on the other hand, does not give the rake's history prior to his meeting Marinda, nor does it follow him into marriage. Count Roderigo's pre-history is given as follows:

> The noble Lord was devoted to his Pleasures, and besides a handsom Person, had an Address and Behaviour that was pleasing to every Body. He did not love his Studies; and there being no War at that time to employ an active Mind, for want of better Business, according to the Custom of *Spain*, he walked up and down the City, wasting his Youth in Trifles, Musick, Masquerades, courting of Ladies, a Form of Devotion which was very common, and fit for such Pilgrims, designing only to conquer, not to be conquered; for as yet all Women equally indifferent to him he had no more Esteem or Tenderness for one than another; his Business was meer [sic] Gallantry, he knew not what it was to love; provided he could but triumph he valued not the Conquest. The whole City rang of his Inconstancy, and yet he was so handsome, so rich, and of such eminent Quality, that he still found a favourable reception amongst the Ladies. each one imagining that her Charms were sufficient to make a Convert of him. His Youth, good Meen, gay Temper and Generosity introduced him every where. Some aspired to gain him for Husband, the already married for a Gallant, and they succeeded the best. Thus he never thought of the Injury he did others, but led a Life of Pleasure, unthinking and without Principles. His Conversation did not lie in the Road of such Persons who either could or cared to teach him. . . . Thus *Roderigo* daily made the Tour of the City of *Valentia* to the Ruin of many an easy Damsel; but that was none of his Concern, for amongst all the Vertues, he was yet wholly unacquainted with that of remorse. (175, 176)

Count Roderigo, is, therefore, the typical rake of the passionate romance, and he behaves accordingly in his relationship with Violenta, before he is "converted" by her. Although Prince S——g's pre-history as a rake is not given, his general attitude is similar to that of Count Roderigo.

The major difference between *Vertue Rewarded* and "The Wife's

Resentment" is, of course, that while one concludes with the marriage of the hero and heroine, the other does not. In "The Wife's Resentment", the heroine is later "ruined" and "abandoned" in spite of being legally married to the hero. Her cries and lamentations on the discovery of her husband's remarriage run to several pages. Finally, she murders her betrayer, showing herself to be not quite as defenceless as the typical ruined and abandoned female. Ironically, one feels, having read "The Wife's Resentment" and numerous other, similar, romances of passion that the author of *Vertue Rewarded* has not given us "the full story" — that the chances of happiness for the prince and princess are slim, given later tradition. Even Richardson's Pamela did not live happily ever after.

Mention of Pamela inevitably brings us to a discussion of the relationship between Richardson's work and *Vertue Rewarded*. For a start, the basic pattern of both *Pamela* and *Vertue Rewarded* appears to be that of the passionate romance, but with a very significant difference in each case. When faced with aggressive and prolonged attacks on her virtue, the typical heroine of passionate romance, as we have already noted, almost invariably succumbs to the male, eventually. This capitulation occurs despite the female's strong-willed, seemingly inflexible resistance. It is against such a background as this that one can appreciate the particular fascination of *Pamela* and, no doubt, *Vertue Rewarded* also, for an eighteenth-century audience. At every stage, almost, of each novel, the contemporary reader must have expected the inevitable rape or seduction of Pamela and Marinda. The more this rape or seduction was postponed, the *more* inevitable it must have seemed next time. But the difference in each of these two cases is that, in spite of all the aggressive as well as benign attempts to overcome the resistance of both Marinda and Pamela, neither loses her honour. In each novel there is also a variation on the pattern of religious romance. Instead of being married to another, or tied to another by binding vows, each of Marinda and Pamela feels she has a grave obligation to herself to preserve her virtue untainted. Both heroines are even prepared to die if that is the alternative to losing their virtue. Pamela declares that she has 'always been taught to value honesty above . . . life'[30] and that she will 'die a thousand deaths rather than be dishonest any way' (i.4). And later she writes to Mr B.: 'Were my *life* in question instead of my *honesty*, I would not wish to involve you or any body in the least difficulty for so worthless a poor creature. . . . Save, then, my innocence, good Heaven! and preserve my mind spotless: and happy shall I be to lay down my worthless life, and see an end to all my troubles and anxieties' (i.137). It is also in a letter that Marinda, in *Vertue Rewarded*, states her case explicitly to the prince, asking him to pardon her rashness towards him since it was 'in defence (of that which I prefer being all things) my Vertue' (160), she says. Earlier, when the Prince has saved Marinda from almost certain death at the hands of bandits, she exclaimed: 'go, leave me to be a prey to them whom thou has hunted away, for I had rather dye here, bemoaning this poor Gentleman who fell in the defence of my Honour, then take refuge with you, who whilst you defend it from others, endeavour to prey upon it your self". (84)

One of the great conflicts in much of eigthteenth-century fiction, in particular in passionate romances, as we have seen, is the conflict in the breast of the heroine between love and duty. The heroine fully appreciates the obligations she owes to her parents in not eloping with, marrying, or, indeed, even consorting in any way with her rakish manfriend. In almost every case, however, the force of love proves much too strong for duty, which is swept aside. A conflict between love and duty is an important feature of both *Pamela* and *Vertue Rewarded*, but the variation is again distinctive. In each case the heroine is in love with her would-be ravisher, and this sets up an obvious conflict between her love for him and her duty to herself and her virtue rather than to her parents. In this conflict, both Pamela and Marinda discover that they harbour within themselves powerful forces which take the side of love, and would overcome duty and give up the citadel of virtue in the cause of love. Pamela, because she believes she has given too obvious an indication of her feelings to Mr B., declares her readiness to 'bite my forward tongue (or rather to beat my more forward heart that dictated to that machine), for what I have said' (i.194). Later, she talks of her willingness to break 'this wicked forward heart of mine' (i.199), which she described as 'treacherous' (i.221), and 'too partial in his [Mr B.'s] favour' (i.220). Likewise, in *Vertue Rewarded*, Marinda says: "if my tell-tale Eyes, or my Countenance has betray'd me, I'll disfigure this Countenance, and tear out these Eyes, rather than they shall invite, or assist, any enterprize, to the prejudice of my Vertue" (33). Later, she admits to the Prince that although a 'Traitor within' (79) takes his part, she has no intention of yielding to him.

While love versus duty is the typical conflict in the breast of the eighteenth-century fictional heroine, a corresponding conflict is taking place in the typical hero, i.e., that between love and ambition and/or interest. The conflict arises when, as is usual, the villain/hero falls in love with a girl who is his inferior in birth and wealth. It is not, therefore, consistent with either his interest or his ambition that he should engage in a marital alliance with such an individual, and thus love, and interest/ambition invariably come into conflict. This is precisely what happens in both *Pamela* and *Vertue Rewarded*; indeed the similarities between the two works are particularly marked in this area. In *Pamela*, the conflict, though fairly explicit throughout the whole work, is commented upon specifically only once, and then only when Mr B. has actually decided to marry Pamela. he says: "I so much value a voluntary love in the person I would wish for my wife, that I would have even prudence and interest hardly named in comparison with it; and can you [Pamela] return me sincerely the honest compliment I now make you? — In the *choice* I have made, it is impossible I should have any view to my interest. Love, *true* love, is the *only* motive by which I am induced"(i, 241). In *Vertue Rewarded*, on the other hand, the reader's attention is specifically directed to the conflict on a number of occasions. In the introduction to the story, the author claims that his (her?) tale will show love, 'triumphant at once over two of these his greatest Enemies, the Noise of War and the Vanity of Ambition" (6). In the story itself, Marinda impersonates a fortune-teller and says to her lover, the Prince: "I fancy your Highness

Introduction

has fallen in love with someone below you, and that your Love and Ambition are at variance". (65) "You guess as right", replies the Prince, "as if you had seen my Heart; and if you can tell me how I shall succeed in my Love, I'll make that, or my Ambition conform itself to the other" (65). Later, the author describes how the Prince, "was so equally divided betwixt Love and Interest, that they governed his breast by turns, sometimes one having the better, and sometimes the other" (79, 80). Finally, when the prince, like Mr B., decides that he will marry his loved one, he says: 'I will no longer indulge this vain Ambition, or let it cross my Love" (161). In each story, therefore, love has had an important victory over interest/ambition.

A good deal of attention in both *Pamela* and *Vertue Rewarded* is also devoted to the disparity in rank between the hero and heroine. This inequality is underlined in the early stages of both novels to suggest, it seems, the improbability of marriage between the hero and heroine,[31] or at least to give some idea of the obstacles in the way of such a marriage. When the Prince's friend and "gentleman of horse", Celadon, is puzzled by a major alteration in humour which he perceives in his master, he says to him: "By your words, Sir, I should guess . . . you are in Love, but the consideration of the place where we are corrects that thought, since in this Island there is scarce one worthy your high Affections' (15). When the prince admits to the violence of his love for Marinda, and considers the possibility of living with her for many years, Celadon retorts: 'why sure . . . your Highness does not design any more than a Jest in't; for though her Person deserves a higher station in the World, yet, since fortune has given her neither Quality nor Riches suitable to it, you are not so prodigal a Lover as *Mark Anthony* was, to quit your Principality, and your Honour besides, for a Mistress" (15). If, as Celadon argues, it would be unbecoming for the prince even to keep Marinda as his mistress, marriage to her seems out of the question. The scene, in the opening pages of *Pamela*, is set in much the same way. Mr B., we are told, "May expect one of the best ladies in the land" (i.7), yet he loves his servant, Pamela, "Better than all the ladies in the land" (i.29). It is unfortunate, we are told, that

xxxii   *Introduction*

Pamela is "so much beneath" (i.30) Mr B.; that if "he knew a lady of birth, just such another as yourself [Pamela], in person and mind, and he would marry her tomorrow" (i.34). The heroines, too, are well aware of their situation and its consequences. Marinda says: 'Nor am I so conceited, as to aim at Marriage [to the Prince]; for what private Gentlewoman could nourish such vain hopes as those of being raised to a Princess? 'Tis more than a bare prodigy, for Earthquakes, Inundations, and those wonders of Nature do sometimes happen; but that a Prince should marry a private maid, is such a wonder, as I never found mentioned in all the Chronicles I have read". (69). Later, she writes to the prince: "your Highness's condescension must not make me forget, that you are a Prince, and that my highest deserts rise no higher than to be the Humblest of your Servants' (89). Pamela, too, is continually preoccupied with Mr B.'s "high degree and my low degree" (i.29), with 'the distance between him [Mr B.] and me" (i.71). As in the case of Marinda, marriage to the man she loves seems beyond the wildest dreams of Pamela. When Mrs Jervis suggests that Mr B. might marry her, Pamela replies: "No, no . . . that cannot be. I neither desire nor expect it. His condition don't permit me to have such a thought" (i.118, 119). The remainder of the novel contains numerous references to this disparity in rank. When Mr B., for instance, offers the possibility of marriage to Pamela, if she lives with him, as his mistress, for a year, Pamela replies: "I have not once dared to look so high as to such a proposal. . . . Your honour, well I know, would not let you stoop to so mean and unworthy a slave as the poor Pamela" (i.167). Later, she describes his regard for her as one "unworthy your condition" (i.189), and, when he eventually hints at marriage, Pamela declares she has "not the presumption to hope such an honour" (i.193).

The hero in each tale is equally preoccupied with the question of rank, and the inequality which exists between him and the woman he loves. Marriage is, of course, the complicating factor: each hero would be only too happy to indulge in a sexual liaison, however lengthy, with his loved one, as long as marriage were not in question. Mr B. describes his passion as having made him "stoop to a meanness" (i.143), and he says to Pamela: "Consider the pride of my condition. I cannot endure the thought of marriage, even with a person of equal or superior degree to myself . . . how then, with the distance between us in the world's judgement, can I think of making you my wife" (i.188). The Prince is even more eloquent on the same topic. Like Mr B., he talks of his "mean passion" (67, 75), and instead of "stooping" he describes himself as having "to cringe to one that was beneath him, and submit himself to one, who could not pretend to a higher Match, than one of his Dependants" (75). Earlier in the story, when the possibility of his marrying Marinda is put to the prince, he replies as follows: "Marriage! . . . why did not I confess to you, that she was a private Gentlewoman, one beneath me? I wonder you should ask such a question. . . . If . . . I can enjoy her on any terms, but those of Marriage, I shall think myself very happy; if not, my Love has so wholly blinded me as to make me forget my Interest and my Honour" (66).

Once marriage has eventually been offered by the male, all the female's problems are over. The male, however, given his previous opposition to marriage, has to make certain psychological adjustments. Each has to arrive at the conclusion that he could not, after all, have possibly married a better woman, and that her qualities and natural breeding are far superior to those of any lady in the land. A good deal of *Pamela* is given over to a proof of the heroine's ladylike qualities *after* Mr B. has proposed marriage, and after the marriage itself. Mr B. now thinks Pamela "would grace a prince" (i.231) and that "No lady in the kingdom can outdo her or better support the condition to which she will be raised" (i.232). The Prince, too, as we noted earlier, reassures himself in the following words: 'You deserve all things, Divine Marinda . . . what Title is too High, or Estate too Magnificent to admit you for a partner! I will no more indulge this vain Ambition or let it cross my Love: tell me *Celadon*, (said he) does not *Marinda*, with her natural Beauty look finer than our Proudest Court Ladies, tho' decked with all their Gaudy Costly Dresses? Yet that lovely Body is but the Shell of a more glorious Inhabitant" (90).

In both *Vertue Rewarded* and *Pamela*, the pattern of

courtship by the male is very similar. Each involuntarily falls in love with the heroine and then makes valiant efforts to rid himself of his "mean" passion. Mrs Jervis is the first to tell us of Mr B.'s attempt to overcome his love for Pamela: "and it is my opinion he finds he can't; and that vexes his proud heart' (i.29), she says. Richardson himself intervenes to tell us that Mr B. had "in vain tried to conquer his passion" (i.76), for Pamela. Mr B. frequently alludes to his struggle also. "In vain, my Pamela, do I struggle against my affection for you" (i.222), he writes. And much earlier he had exclaimed: "I, in spite of my heart, and all the pride of it, cannot but love you . . . I love you to extravagance" (i.69). Equally, in *Vertue Rewarded*, the Prince realises, too late, that he has been irrevocably hooked by love. The author tells us that the Prince "had no power to over-awe or check his Love, or Relations to controul it" (27). Later, the Prince describes his love for Marinda as "one so violent, and yet so unreasonable, that I am unable to curb it, nor have I any hopes of success, if I let it go on" (64). Yet, he resolves to "shake off the mean Passion; but all his endeavours were vain; the more he tried it, the more sensible he grew, how unable he was to perform it" (67). The only antidote for the violence of Mr B.'s and the Prince's passion is to enjoy the heroine. "I will have her" (i.46), Mr B. says to Mrs Jervis: and to Pamela herself, he later says: "I must have you" (i.188). The Prince, too, "some way or other is resolved to enjoy Marinda (16), and "cannot endure the thoughts of losing her" (67). Nor is the anguish of the male, in his inability to enjoy the female, a mental one only: both heroes are actually in danger of death in their respective stories, and the possibility of losing the female forever is given as a major contributory factor. Mr B. becomes "very ill indeed' (i.226), when Pamela leaves him, yet recovers immediately she returns. On her return to him, at his request, Mr B. says to Pamela: "Life is not life without out! Had you refused me, and I had hardly hopes you would oblige me, I should have had a severe fit of it, I believe" (i.227). Celadon, in *Vertue Rewarded*,[32] accuses Marinda of endangering the life of the Prince by her cruelty, i.e. by her refusal to have anything further to do with him. He prevails upon

Introduction   xxxv

Marinda to write to the prince, and then uses her letter to "cure his Body, by this sovereign Ballsom which he brought for his mind" (89). The balsam works, eventually, and the Prince, like Mr B., is restored to health. In each story, therefore, the love of the hero is so violent that it causes severe mental and physical distress, bringing him, we are led to believe, close to death. The heroine in each story, however, refuses to provide the necessary relief by being enjoyed unlawfully, and the dilemma is only resolved when Mr B. and the Prince agree to pay the ultimate prince — marriage — as a cure for their ailment.

The deceptions practised by Mr B. and the prince in order to beguile Pamela and Marinda are of a kind also. Mr B. pretends he's going to marry someone other than Pamela; later, he has plans for a bogus marriage ceremony with Pamela. He hides in a closet, disguises himself, pretends he is gone on a journey to Stamford, all with the intention of effecting the rape of Pamela. In *Vertue Rewarded*, the prince's first stratagem is reminiscent of Mr B.'s pretended journey to Stamford. He organizes a ball, and hopes to lure Marinda to it by pretending that he himself has gone to Dublin. He rides out of Clonmel, but returns secretly in time for the ball. The remaining deceptions in the story are carried out on the prince's behalf by Celadon — disguise, a pretence that the prince will marry Marinda, then a pretence that he is already married.

In several other details, also, there is an obvious similarity between *Pamela* and *Vertue Rewarded*. Both heroines are concerned, for example, that the acknowledgement of their love for the hero will lead to inevitable ruin;[33] both attempt to escape from their lovers and almost die in the process;[34] each story concerns itself a good deal with "terms" either honourable or dishonourable;[35] and each heroine assumes that if she accedes to dishonourable terms that she will be abandoned as soon as her lover grows tired of her;[36] the dream of Marinda in *Vertue Rewarded*,[37] as well as recalling the dream of Pamela,[38] is strikingly similar to two of the attempts at rape in *Pamela*;[39] the heroes too, as well as being anonymous, share a preoccupation about rivals for the love of their sweethearts.[40] One detail which deserves particular attention is the ending of *Vertue Rewarded* and the corresponding event in *Pamela*, i.e. her marriage to Mr B. Marinda is described as having "received the reward of her invincible Vertue, in Loving and being Beloved, and in having gained a Prince, who raised her Quality as high (in comparison of what she was before) as a Woman's Ambition could desire" (103).[41] Pamela, for her part, thanks providence, "which has, through so many incricate mazes, made me tread the path of innocence, and so amply rewarded me for what it has enabled me to do." (i.241, 242). Another feature of *Pamela* which is particularly interesting, though one would hesitate to place too much emphasis on it, is the use of the words "prince", and "princess" in the story. Early in the novel, Pamela, in objecting to the liberties Mr B. has taken with her, exclaims: "Yet, Sir, I will be bold to say, I am honest, though poor: and if you was a prince, I would not be otherwise" (i.12). Later, she claims that her soul, if not her body, "is of equal importance with the soul of a princess . . ." (i.137). Mr B. takes up the refrain when he says to Pamela, after he has proposed to her: "You would grace a prince, my fair one". (231)

Mark Kinkead-Weekes in his preface to the Everyman Library edition of *Pamela*, refers to what he sees as a serious failure in the novel:

The most central failure . . . concerns not Pamela but B. Once one has learned to read with the sensitivity to implications that Richardson demands, it becomes clear that after markedly crude beginnings B. does become a complex character in the grip of acute conflict. But if Pamela and B. are both on the stage, and we are required to understand and judge them both in their opposition, the fact remains that we live always in her mind and never in his because the novel is told from a single point of view. Not only is it fatally easy to miss the exact fluctuations of B's conflict through superficial reading, but we inhabit so continuously a mind in which he appears simply as a "black-hearted wretch" that we tend to oversimplify him too. (It is always a danger in point-of-view writing that we are tempted to adopt the viewpoint of one character instead of holding them all against our own greater knowledge). At important points we need the same direct experience of B's heart and mind that we have of

Pamela's; but the single focus cannot provide this. The result is dangerous when we come to B.'s reformation.[42]

A notable feature of *Vertue Rewarded* is that in spite of its being written from the point of view of a single character — the Prince — the author cleverly seeks to avoid the dangers associated with this technique. At important points we *do* have direct experience of Marinda's heart, in spite of the single focus. On two vital occasions,[43] the Prince overhears conversations between Marinda and her confidante, Diana. Later, he agrees to allow Celadon to impersonate a fortune-teller in a successful attempt to induce Marinda to reveal her inmost thoughts.[44] Celadon is important in another way, too. He is courting Diana, Marinda's confidante, and uses his position continually to gain additional information as to the state of Marinda's heart. In spite of the novel's single point-of-view narration, therefore, the author has managed to convey a "double vision". The narrative technique of *Pamela* is, however, very similar to that of *Vertue Rewarded* in one way. A feature of *Pamela* is Mr B.'s continual awarenes of the state of Pamela's feelings towards him, because of his access to her "heart" in the various ways described. In both stories the heroine is unaware, for quite some time, of the extent of her lover's knowledge. After Mr B.'s proposal of marriage, Pamela agrees to let him have any letters he may not have already seen. This is, interestingly, paralleled in *Vertue Rewarded* by Marinda's having Diana "acquaint the Prince with all she knew of her [Marinda's] thoughts, without disguising anything" (99).

There appears to be little similarity between the characters of Marinda and Pamela, yet they are quite alike in one way, i.e. in the way each is mesmerised by the man who is out to "enjoy" her in whatever way possible. Marinda freely admits to being captivated by the prince and his charms; Pamela never does, at least not until her marital prospects are almost assured. Each tries to escape from her lover, but it is more than physical bondage that is involved, as each learns. Each story, then, features a peculiar combination of attraction and repulsion. One major difference between the two stories lies in the area of sexuality. The Prince never actually attempts either to seduce or rape Marinda, though it appears he would attempt either in his effort to enjoy her. Marinda, for her part, is certainly apprehensive of such a possibility, and her confidante, Diana, warns her explicitly as follows: "Have a care *Marinda* . . . that you do not engage too far with one who is so much above you; 'tis not safe Intriguing with Persons of his Quality; Inferiour Lovers may be jested with as long as we please, and thrown off at will, but such as he seldom leave us without carrying away our Vertue, or at least our Reputation: And you will too late curse your own Charms when they have exposed you to be ruined (like a young Conjurer) by raising a Spirit which you are not able to lay'. (33) *Pamela*, on the other hand, is a typical novel of procrastinated rape or seduction, with a continual emphasis on the prurient.

Having considered in some detail the resemblances between *Pamela* and *Vertue Rewarded*, one basic issue still remains to be explored, viz. whether or not Richardson ever actually read *Vertue Rewarded*. I hope I have already given a strong indication that he did, but there is also further evidence to be examined. The repetition of the title of the 1693 work in the subtitle of *Pamela* deserves some attention, for instance. While this repetition might obviously be ascribed to simple coincidence, it is worth noting that no other work of fiction prior to 1740, so far as I am aware, contained "vertue rewarded" in its title or subtitle. Another fact merits notice, also, though, perhaps, at the risk of seeming too obvious, i.e., that Richardson *could* have read *Vertue Rewarded*, given that it was published in 1693. Richardson's most recent biographers, Eaves and Kimpel, point out that he was "inclined to deny"[45] that he had ever read other works of fiction. They are sceptical of Richardson's claim, however, and explain it as follows: "We suspect that he did like the idea of being first in the field and did not want anyone to think him indebted to the French or anyone else."[46] In spite of his being inclined to deny having read fiction, Richardson became a printer in the first place because he thought it a profession which would gratify his "Thirst after Reading".[47] More interesting still, are the following remarks by Richardson in a letter of 1753: "As a bashful and not forward Boy, I was an early Favourite with all the young

Women of Taste and Reading in the Neighbourhood. Half a Dozen of them when met to work with their Needles, used, when they got a Book they liked, and thought I should, to borrow me to read to them."[48] It is obviously not inconceivable that *Vertue Rewarded* was one of the books Richardson was asked to read to the needleworkers. The title, *Vertue Rewarded*, certainly seems to suggest a book which might appeal to young ladies of "taste and reading": equally, it would appear not to be one which would offend the susceptibilities of a young boy — even a young Richardson.

One final problem remains to be addressed, i.e. Richardson's claim that *Pamela* was actually based on a true story told to him by a gentleman with whom he was "intimately acquainted".[49] Intriguingly, the anonymous author of *Vertue Rewarded* makes an identical claim as follows, in his "Preface to the Ill-natured Reader": "know, that the main Story is true, I heard of a Gentleman who was acquainted with the Irish princess, and knew all the Intrigue, and having from him so faithful a relation of it, I make the scene the very same where it was transacted, the time the same, going on all the way with the Truth, as far as conveniency would permit; I only added some few Circumstances, and interlined it with two or three other Stories for variety sake" (3). One would hesitate to attach any significance to this claim, it is so typical of writers of fiction at that time. Yet Samuel Richardson's claim has never been doubted. Perhaps this is because his relation of the original Pamela story[50] bears the stamp of a true tale. Yet a significant discrepancy remains. In one of his letters[51] Richardson claims that he heard the story around 1716, and, in another,[52] that he heard it in 1725. One other piece of this jigsaw is, perhaps, contained in this well-known passage from one of Richardson's letters: "I recollect that I was early noted for having Invention. I was not fond of Play as other Boys: My Schoolfellows used to call me *Serious* and *Gravity*: and five of them particularly delighted to single me out, either for a walk, or at their Father's Houses or at mine, to tell them Stories, as they phrased it. Some I told them from my Readings as true; others from my Head as mere Invention".[53] It is not, surely, inconceivable, that *Pamela* was written from Richardson's "reading as true", while *Clarissa*, on the other hand, was written from his "Head as mere Invention". Perhaps the most plausible explanation for the genesis of *Pamela* may be that it is a unique amalgam, formed from a synthesis of the true story Richardson once heard and a not dissimilar fictitious story, *Vertue Rewarded*, which he had once read. Most important of all, perhaps, *Vertue Rewarded* provided the general narrative technique and framework for *Pamela*. In this context, it is intriguing to note Eaves and Kimpel speculating on the various causes "for the collapse of *Pamela* about half way through part one".[54] In the light of my remarks so far, one obvious reason for this so-called collapse proffers itself immediately. *Vertue Rewarded* ends almost immediately after the Prince's offer of marriage. Could one not reasonably argue that it is when Mr B. offers marriage that *Pamela* starts to collapse, i.e. after the model has ceased to provide guidance?

One hopes that on the basis of both internal and external evidence, *Vertue Rewarded* has been shown to be a credible source for *Pamela*. It can be stated, with little qualification, that there is no other work of English fiction quite like either in the fictionally-fertile half century 1690–1740. Given that it was published forty-seven years before *Pamela*, *Vertue Rewarded* is, in its own way, as exceptional a work as Richardson's. It appeared long before the vogue of either passionate or religious romance, yet *Vertue Rewarded* appears to be a fascinating synthesis created from both forms, but without the sensuality of one or the sermonising of the other. *Pamela* is a later synthesis of the passionate and religious romance, and while Richardson avoids the excesses of each, he is obviously guilty of the lesser charge of gratuitously highlighting both sex and sermon.

The text which follows seeks to reproduce the 1693 edition of *Vertue Rewarded* as faithfully as possible. There are no paragraphs in the original and these have been introduced into the present edition for ease of reading. The somewhat clumsy seventeenth-century method of indicating dialogue by means of inverted commas down either side of the page has been dropped in favour of the more conventional, modern method. Where necessary, words dropped by the original typesetter have been added, in parenthesis, to the text to make the author's intended meaning clear. Otherwise, all syntactical, grammatical and spelling errors have been reproduced.

Hubert McDermott
University College, Galway

Vertue Rewarded;
OR, THE
IRIS H Princeſs.
A NEW
NOVEL.

She ne're ſaw Courts, yet Courts could have undone
with untaught Looks, and an unpractiſ'd Heart;
Her Nets, the moſt prepar'd, could never ſhun,
For Nature ſpread them in the ſcorn of Art.
Gond. lib. 2. Cant. 7.

LONDON,

Printed for *R. Bentley,* at the Poſt-houſe in *Ruſſel-ſtreet,* in *Covent-Garden.* 1693.

THE

Dedicatory Epistle

To the Incomparable

MARINDA

Madam,

THIS Novel throws it self at your Feet, and pays you Homage as its Master's Representative: It has been the product of some leisure hours, and will I hope do me this second kindness, to divert you in the Reading, as it did me in the Making. I need not, as others, give any reason for the Dedication, since to be made by me, is sufficient to entitle it yours: But that is not the only claim it can lay to your Favour; for in describing the *Marinda* of this Novel, I borrow from you, not only her Name, but some of the chief Beauties I adorn her with: Though you may imagine she had no mean ones of her own, since (being but a private Gentlewoman) she could by their help alone make so sudden a Conquest over the Heart of a Prince, who had certainly (in so many Courts as he had been in) seen very agreeable Faces, set off with the additional Splendor of Quality, yet none of them had that effect over him, which hers gained without those advantages. Besides, her true Character suits very well with you: She was an Innocent Country Virgin, ignorant of the Intrigues and Tricks of the Court Ladies; her Vertue, like yours, untainted and undecayed, needed none of their Artificial Embellishments to guild it over; and that Innocence which appears eminently in both of you, as little wants these Ladies

Artifices to set it off, as you do their *Fucus*[55] for your Faces; since true Innocence is as far beyond Dissimulation, as your Colour is beyond all the Paint of the Town; in both of these you give Nature as signal a Triumph over Art, as ever she had in any two things whatsoever. I wish I could liken you to her in one thing more; that is, That your Servant were of as high Quality as hers; but this wish is made meerly for your sake: For to me, as you are more precious than a Crown, so is the Title of a Prince inferiour to that Glorious one, of being the

Humblest of your Servants.

The PREFACE

TO THE

Ill-Natur'd READER.

THe Dutchess of Suffolk, entertaining once at her Table the Bloody Bonner,[56] Bishop of London, sate first by the Duke her Husband, but the Duke removing her thence, she went and sate by the Bishop, saying, That since she could not sit by him she loved best, she would next him she loved worst: So dear dogged Reader, from writing an Epistle to her I love best, like the Dutchess, I change and remove to you whom I love worst; for Writers hate none so much as Ill-natured Readers: Perhaps you'll ask, why then this Epistle to you whom I hate, and not rather to the Good-natured? Why for the same reason that the Dutchess sate by Bonner, meerly to pass my Jest on you; though another may be given, which is, That since Prefaces were partly designed to make the Reader Indulgent and Favourable to the Book he is going to read, there's no need of a Preface to others, since the Good-Natured will be kind to it of themselves; but 'tis you, that put us to the trouble of Prefacing. Therefore to indear it the more to you know, that the main Story is true, I heard of a Gentleman who was acquainted with the Irish Princess, and knew all the Intrigue, and having from him so faithful a Relation of it, I made the Scene the very same where it was transacted, the time the same, going on all the way with the Truth, as far as conveniency would permit; I only added some few Circumstances, and interlined it with two or three other Stories, for variety sake, which is as necessary to the setting off the true Relation, and making it pleasant, especially to you nice Readers, as Sauces are to the dressing up a Dish of Meat, to provoke the sickly

Appetite it is design'd for. I Printed it for the ease of her whom it was made for; if you like it, much good may it do you; if you will not believe it, you have Liberty of Conscience; but whether you believe, or disbelieve, like, or dislike, is indifferent to me, since in such a trivial thing as this, I no more fear discredit by writing a bad one, than I could hope for Fame in writing it well. But I believe you are eager to see what is in the Book, and therefore I'll detain you no longer.

Farewell.

Vertue Rewarded;

OR, THE

IRISH Princess

AS that mighty River which overflows Ægypt, and, with its prevailing Torrent, often drowns those Provinces, which Nature only designed it to water, yet proceeds at first from such mean beginnings, that most Geographers have been unable to trace it to its Spring: So Loves swifter and more violent Stream has its first rise from such small Channels, such trifling circumstances, that the Heart itself can scarce perceive its Original; nay very often does not discern its progress, till it is too strong for it, and so the sudden vigour of its Torrent surprizes the unwary Lover, just as the *Zudder* Sea, driven with a North west Wind, breaks the Diques, and overwhelms the drowzy *Hollander*, before he suspects any danger. Yet so Natural is Self-conceit, and so Universal our pretence to Knowledge, that few there are who will be so Modest, as to own themselves wholly Ignorant of any thing which you shall ask them a Reason for. Hence it is, that, among other things, Love too is understood by all, and not one but will give his Verdict of it as soon as you ask him: The States-man will tell you it is caused by want of Ambition; the Merchant for want of Self-Interest; the Souldier for want of Action, and a thirst after Honour; and the Scholar will prove to you that 'tis gotten by Idleness: But it is with this, as with the Philosophers Stone, whose mysterious Nature all guess at, and none know what it is, for it very often breaks all the Rules that are prescribed against it: Sets upon the States-man at Court, and overcomes his Ambition; seizes on the Merchant in his Counting-House, and weighs down his Interest; finds the Scholar in his Study, and teaches him a new System of Philosophy, which baffles all the old; wounds the daring Souldier, even when he is clad in Steel, and makes him tamely submit to Captivity, in the very midst of his Conquests: The Story that I am going to relate will be an excellent proof of this, being an Instance of an extraordinary sort: It makes Love triumphant at once over two of these his greatest Enemies, the Noise of War, and the Vanity of Ambition: and shows you a Prince of great Valour, guarded equally by both of these, could not defend himself from the Powerful Eyes of a Forreigner, and one as far beneath him in Quality, as Love afterwards placed her above him, when he lay at her feet imploring her Mercy.

When our present King had fought the Battel at the *Boyn*, and drove the Routed Enemy into *Limerick*, he endeavoured to root up the War, by Reducing that obstinate City, that durst hold out alone against the force of three Kingdoms, united in a Royal Army; he had then amongst his Forreign Troops several petty Princes, who fought under him; some as volunteers, to learn the Art of War under so Great, so Experienced a Master; some as Souldiers of Fortune, who thought by their Valour to recommend themselves to his Favour, and obtain by that means some Important Charge in the Army, the Honour and Profit of which might exalt and maintain them suitable to those High Characters, which their Titles deserved. Among the latter sort may be reckon'd the Prince of S———*g*, the smallness of whose Principality not affording him an Income agreeable to his High Title, and Higher Mind, he was resolved to acquire that Plenty which his Fortune had denied him, and show by his Valour, that he was nothing beholding to her for giving him Titles, but rather that she was unkind, in not giving him as plentiful a Revenue, as suited with the largeness of his Heart, and the vaster extent of his Merit. To this intent he came over Sea in a small Command, if we consider him as a Prince, though in a Post eminent enough to give him some occasions of publishing his Valour;

'twas in this Station he was, when our Forces were from all parts drawing together to invest *Limerick,* in order to which our Prince was to march through *Clonmell,* a City in the County of *Tipperary,* scituated in a large Plain near the *Sewer,* now grown obscure, formerly famous for the great Battel fought just by it, between two Brothers who were Competitors for the Crown of *Mounster;* when that famous Island had five Crowned Heads to Govern its Inhabitants.

It was the Chief Street of this Town our Prince was marching through, on Horse-back, at the Head of his Men, bowing low to both sides, which were fill'd all along with People, who crowded thither to see those Arms which were to secure them from the Enemies of their Liberty and Religion; when lifting up his Eyes towards the Windows, which were fill'd with the chief Gentry of the City, he espied in one of them a Beauty which fixed his sight, as if she alone were worthy his Attention: He continued looking that way, and turned not his Eyes off the Window, till the fieryness of his Horse (which could not indure to stand still) had carried him beyond the House, and left the delightful Prospect behind him; and afterwards he was so wholly taken up with the thoughts of what he had seen, that he rode on without regarding which way, till one of his Officers rode up, and told him that his Highness was past the House which was designed him for his Lodging: The P. at this began to recollect himself, and giving Orders concerning the good Behaviour of his Souldiers, gave them leave to repair to several Quarters, whilst he by the Head Officers was Conducted to his; after some Ceremonies past they repaired to their rest, and left the Prince at liberty to take as much of his, as the inquietude of his Thoughts would permit him.

He found himself tired with Travelling, and desirous of rest, yet incapable of taking any; He found his Thoughts much disorder'd, and went to Bed to see whether Sleep would compose them: His Soul, like the Bodies of those that have the Rheumatism, seemed very weary; yet as their Limbs are still uneasie, though on the softest Beds, so was his Mind; and coveted sleep as much as their Limbs do rest, and could as little obtain it.

O Love, thou most dangerous Distemper of the Soul! most dangerous because we do not perceive Thee, till Thou art too far gone to be cured: Thou subtle Enemy! who takest the strongest Hearts, because Thou always usest Surprise: and undermining our Reason, never appearest in the light, till Thou art too far enter'd to be driven out: 'Twas thus, Treacherous Deity, Thou didst overcome our Prince, by attacking him when he least was aware of Thee; he little feared Hostility in a Town which he enter'd as a Friend; nor did he expect that one, and that of the weaker Sex, should offer him Violence at the head of his Battalion.

He suspected the true Cause so little, that he wonder'd at his own inquietude, and could not imagine what it was that could keep him awake on a soft Bed, who used to sleep so sound in the Camp on a hard Quilt, and often on the Ground: However, awake he lay all night, and did not once close his Eyes, till day-light shone in at his Window: At the Sun's first appearance he got up, quite weary of his Bed, where he had the worst Nights rest he ever took in his Life; for though he had indured the hardship of many a cold night in Winter Camps; yet they all seemed easie and pleasant, in comparison of this one Night's Fatigue; for all the thoughts in those Camps of Blood and War, the dread of a neighbouring Enemy, and the next day's Battel, were not so troublesome to his Repose, as those of his coming into this Town: The whole Scene of his entrance intruded into his Thoughts; the Noise and Hurry of the People was still in his Ears; and the Window, and the Charming Spectator that looked out of it, seemed still before his Eyes: Though he scarce mistrusted that it was gone so far with him, as to be in Love; yet he was very desirous to come in Company with that beautiful Stranger, who had been so much it his Thoughts, and to satisfie himself whether she was really so Lovely, as she appeared at a distance: But neither knowing her Name, nor the place where she lived, he imagined that nothing but accident could bring him to a second sight of her; but as he was musing upon the difficulty of finding her out, *Celadon*, the Gentleman of his Horse, came to bid him Good-morrow, and acquainted him,

That two or three great Officers were below, waiting for admittance to speak with him: The Prince, who was glad of anything that might be an amusement to his troubled Mind, sent for them up, and received them with a great deal of Civility: After the first Complements, the Prince told them, He had Orders to await the King's coming to the Town; and after some discourse of the Progress of Affairs in general, they began to talk of the pleasure of Company, and how they should spend those few days which they were to pass in the Town: One proposed Training the Souldiers, another the Tavern, and the Third a Consort of Musick; and when every one had past their Votes, the Prince bad *Celadon* give his: This *Celadon* was a young brisk *English* Cavalier, of a small Stature, but a Soul sufficiently Great, and which disdain'd to think that the littleness of his Body made him inferior to any one, either in open Valour in the Field, or the management of an Intrigue at home: And certainly never was any ones Humour more equally divided, between Love and War, than his: He was an exact Volunteer in both, and as he would hazard his Person any time, and fight for him that would give him the best Promotion, so was he no less a Souldier of Fortune in Love than War; would change his side often, offer his Service to every Lady that would accept of it, and still was most hers, who was readiest to reward him: He was the Younger Brother of a good Family; and having gone into Forreign Camps for a Livelihood, he had by his Courage, Wit, and Good Fortune, raised himself so high into the Prince's favour, as to be made his Gentleman of Horse; he being to speak in his turn, told the Prince, That since they had left him a deciding Vote, he was for trying each of them by turns; and if they would begin with the Musick first, he would add to it one of his own most delighting Divertisements, the Company of Women; and to that purpose, if the Prince pleased to be that Night at the Ball, he would take care to invite all the young Gentry of the Town to it: The Prince told him he was the same he always thought him; that *Celadon* that took Love to be as important an Affair of Life, as either Eating or Drinking, and accordingly provided for it as carefully; this raillery brought on other discourse, which lasted while *Celadon* went to make preparations for the Ball; at last he came back and told them that all things were ready, and the Company invited.

On one side of the Town stood a large Country House, which though not built after the *Dorick* Order, or the exacter neatness of Courtly Lodgings, yet its largeness gave liberty to guess at the Magnificence and Hospitality of the Owner: It belonged to the Great *Moracho*,[57] famous all over the Kingdom for his Riches, particularly in his flocks of Sheep, as numerous as those of the mighty *Scythian*,[58] whose son was the Terror of the World; or that Rich Man of the East, whom the *Turkish* Chronicles make Steward to *Alexander* the Great: All his Ground, far and near, was thick covered with his fleecy Wealth: You would have thought by their bleatings that you were in *Arcadia*, and Shepherdism coming in fashion again:' Twas this House which was pitched upon for the Ball; and what place so fit for Dancing and innocent Mirth, as a spacious Hall, whose Building, Size, and Furniture, altogether rustical, imprinted such lively Idea's of Country Freedom, and Country Innocence: Hither *Celadon* conducted our Prince and his Martial Company; their Musick was as good as the Town could afford, and their Reception suitable to the Riches and Hospitality of him that entertain'd them.

The Prince, who went thither, rather to shun his former thoughts, than out of any inclination to the Company, or the Dancing, sat by, a Looker-on: Some of the Officers who were not so seriously bent, took out those whose Face, Meen, or Shape pleased them the best, and in their several Dances either shewed their Skill, or at least pleased themselves with the conceit that they did so.

Celadon, who always employed such a time as this well, was not idle now; but gazed on one, talked to another, bowed to the third, and left none of the Ladies unregarded; and as a cunning Hound, when he comes among a Herd of Deer, singles out the best, and never changes Scent, till he runs him down. so our skillful Hunter, who knew all the Mazes, Turnings, and Doublings in the course of Love, ranged through all the Company of the fairer Sex, till he lighted on the handsomest. He would not leave her, till he had prevailed with her to be his Partner in a Country Dance; and tho' till she was drawn out few observed her, because either Chance, or her own Modesty had placed her in a dark part of the Room, yet when she came into the light, she alone drew the admiration of all Men, as she did the envy of the Women:

Her face was oval and somewhat thin, as if grief had but newly left it, yet her looks were as chearful, as if it had not left the least impression on her mind; some signs of the Small-pox were just perceivable, yet they and her thinness, instead of lessening, served rather to increase the repute of her Beauty, while they shew'd how it had triumphed over those two great destroyers of the handsomest Faces: Her Forehead was high and smooth, as if no Frown had ever deformed it to a wrinkle; and as much beyond the whiteness of the rest of her Sex, as theirs is beyond the browner Complexion of ours; her Neck, and all the parts of her Face were equally Snowy, except her Cheeks; but they, as if they received their colour from the Rays which her Eyes darted down on them, were of such a lively Carnation, as if that and the rest of her Face were at a strife, which of those two Colours were the best. Her Eyes were of the same azure of the clearest Summer Skyes, and, like them too, so shining, that it would dazle you to look on them, and her Brows, which grew over them in an exact Arch, were inclining to a light colour, as if they got it from the brightness of those Beams which shone from beneath them. Her Stature was neither so low at that Sex usually is, nor so tall as to seem too masculine; her Shape was curiously slender, and all her Limbs after a feminine delicacy, but she had withall a Deportment so Great and so Majestick, that the comeliness of the stronger Sex was mixed with the graces of the weaker: And that the stateliness of her Carriage seemed to command that Love and Adoration, which the sweetness of her Face did invite to.

I will not describe how she was drest, let those Ladies be set off with such helps, who like Peacocks owe their Pride to their Feathers; hers were no part of her Beauty, they were put on for Modesty, not for Ornament; and served her as Clouds do the Sun, to screen her more glorious Beauties from the Eyes of weak

Mankind, who would else be as infallibly ruined by the sight of the one, as by the excessive heat of the other. The Prince, who sate looking on the Dance, no sooner saw her, but he knew her to be the same whom he had seen in the Window, and whom he so much longed to come acquainted with, he was overjoy'd that he had gotten an opportunity he so little expected; he was so eager to speak to her, and so impatient till the Dance was over, that any one who had observed him might easily have perceived it: As soon as the Dance was ended, he call'd to *Celadon*, and telling him that he could not but be weary, proffered to supply his place: *Celadon*, with a great deal of submission told him, that he was willing to resign any place to his Highness, and so sate down: In the mean time a Tune began, and the Lady waited for her Partner; but when she saw the Prince come, she blush'd, and desired his Highness would pardon her, if she pray'd him to chuse another, because she was weary: The Prince would not allow of that excuse; but when she Danced several times wrong, and put the Company out, and was out of Countenance her self, he thought her blushing proceeded from her not understanding the Dance, and so accepted the excuse, and sate down with her. Having a mind to discourse with her, and not having so good a command of the *English* tongue, he spoke to her in *French,* and asked her, did she understand him? she answered him again in the same Language:

"Sir, I have just such a smattering of it as you have of *English*, but your Highness shows me so wise a President,[59] of not venturing to discourse in a Language which I cannot express my self well in, that I ought to follow it, and dare no more speak *French* to your Highness, than you will *English* to me."

"Madam," *said the Prince,* "though you speak the *French* Tongue so prettily, that one does not know which becomes your Mouth better, that, or your own, yet e're a one of them is thrown away on you; for that tempting Face speaks so much of it self, that had Nature ty'd up your Tongue, yet your Looks alone have power enough to lead all Mankind astray, and draw them more attractively after you by their Eyes, than the most perswading Eloquence can by the Ears."

"Sir," *replyed the Lady*, "Had your Highness made these Compliments to some celebrated Beauty, custom would have prepared her an Answer; but to one that is so unused to them as I am, they come so unexpected, that I must desist Discoursing, as I did just now from Dancing, not so much because I am weary of it, as because I do not know how to go on; and really, with us Country Maids, our Tongues walk like our Feet, and as our Country Dances follow an easie methodical way, so does our Talk; whilst your Court Wit, like your dances, are so made up of Art in one place, a cunning Jest, or a hard Step in another; your Fancies, like your Feet, do caper so high, and are so nimble, that our plainness seems ridiculous in both, and yours is so difficult to us, that it gives us no hope of ever arriving to as much as a faint imitation."

"Dancing", *said the Prince*, "was design'd in imitation of Courtship, the Ladies flying off from the Man to shew her Coyness; her sometimes coming forward, and sometimes retiring, her Inconstancy; and their meeting at last signifies their Marriage; now if the Fashion be here as 'tis in our Country, to kiss at last, i'faith, Madam, I'll leave Poets and Dancing-Masters to shew their Skill in Talking and Dancing, and care not how unskillfully I go in either, so that I may be sure of my reward in the end":

"If you go no farther than a bare kiss," *replyed the Lady smiling*, "few would refuse your Highness that reward, to have the honour of Dancing with you; but if you carry on the Simile so far as to relate to Marriage, your Highness should consider, that the sport of Courtship, like that of Dancing, is quite gone when it comes to the kiss; and no more pleasure remains afterwards to the poor tired Dancers, than that of thinking it over again; for them, as an old saying of ours has it, our dancing days are gone."

As she spoke these words, the Dance ended, and some of the Company coming up to hearken to their discourse, the Lady rose from her Seat, and took her leave; the Prince could neither persuade her to stay, nor to give him leave to wait on her home; then he desired to know where she lived, but she begg'd his Pardon: The Prince, who was resolved to know her, sent his

Page to observe her, and to take notice where she lodged, and so fell in talk with the other Company, continuing it with one or other, till the lateness of the night broke up the Ball, and sent every one to his several home; the Prince had not been long at his, e're the Page came and brought him word, that he had housed the Lady in the High-street, that she lived there with a Gentlewoman who was her Mother-in-law:

The Prince who was so uneasie before, and so desirous to see her, since he had that interview he wished for, began to be more at ease, though more in Love than before, and whereas his thoughts were formerly distracted several ways, now they ran all on her; the Ball, the Dancing, and all the rest of the Entertainment was as faintly remembered, as if he had only seen them a Dream; but what she had said or done, was as fresh, as if it were that very moment acting over again: One while he fancied he saw her dancing, another, that he saw with what a grace she spake, and every word of her discourse was as ready in his memory, as if it were the only ones engraven there; no wonder if those who will not give credit to the Stories of Apparitions, say, the Persons are deluded by the excess of Fear, and the strength of their own Fancies, for the force of imagination is as strong in Love as it is in Fear, and makes the cheated Amourist still think he sees the Fair one, and though she be an hundred mile off, yet her Face, her Ayr, her Meen, and every thing that formerly pleased his sights, seems still to dance before it: and as the guilty Conscience of the Murderer presents the Fantom of the Murdered to his view, so Lovers are haunted with Spectres too, only the Murderers appear in a dreadful, the Lovers in a pleasing Form.

This night had our Prince several of these delightful Visions, which were so intruding, that neither his Reason could banish them while he was awake, nor Sleep free him from them in his Dreams; as soon as he waked he sent for *Celadon*, and having ordered him to shut the Door, and sit down on his Bed-side, he spake thus to him.

"When you went with me to the Emperour's Court, do you remember how many excellent Beauties we saw there? What variety too, Black, Brown, and Light, yet all fair to Perfection; you may remember how indifferent I was to them all, that I never threw away an hours discourse on them, unless it were to rally the Pride, the Hypocrisie, the Ambition, and the other Vanities which that Sex is given to; and then though I seem'd in Jest, yet I took what I spake to be the truth, nor did I think that the low opinion I had of Woman-kind would ever let me shew them any regard beyond bare Complaisance: But I was deceived, for I have in these two days had a greater alteration in my humour, than I believed my whole life could produce."

"By your words, Sir, I should guess", said *Celadon*, "that you are in Love, but the consideration of the place where we are corrects that thought, since in this island there is scarce one worthy your high Affections."

"I wish you could perswade me to that," *reply'd the Prince;* "but will not you recant your own Opinion, when I recall to your mind the Beautiful Partner you last Night danced with?"

"The young Gentlewoman", *reply'd he,* "had as large a stock of Beauty, as the most Romantick Lover can either wish or imagine in a Mistress; and indeed, if your Highness has a mind to Intrigue away this Winter that's coming on, I could not wish you a pleasanter than she is likely to make, if her Wit be answerable to her Beauty":

"By what small tryal I have had of her," *answered the Prince,* "I believe it falls very little short of it; and if my Love for her encreases a little longer, at the same rate as it has done since its birth, I fear 'twill out-live more Campaigns with me, than I shall Winters with her":

"Why sure," *said* Celadon, "your Highness does not design any more than a Jest in't; for though her Person deserves a higher station in the World, yet, since Fortune has given her neither Quality nor Riches suitable to it, you are not so prodigal a Lover as *Mark Anthony* was, to quit your Principality, and your Honour besides, for a Mistress:"

"There's no need of that," *said the Prince,* "don't lay such Blockadoes in my way to her; for be it ever so long, or difficult, I will use both Patience and Diligence to overcome it; for some way or other I am resolved to enjoy her; and if you will assist me, I shall not think all that ever I can do for you will make you too large a recompense."

"Your Highness", *said* Celadon, "never yet gave me an opportunity to shew my diligence in serving you; but if you please to tell me how you intend to bring this about, I will follow your directions to the utmost of my Power":

"All that I would desire of you at present," *said the Prince,* "is to make me an *English* Song, because I am not will enough acquainted with the Tongue; and make it to the Tune we heard sung to Count *Epithalamium,* and with your Violin and my Guittar we'll go this Night and Serenade her":

"I'll take my leave of you now," *said* Celadon, "and in the Afternoon I'll wait on you with the Song."

Celadon fail'd not his promise, but came in the Evening, and sat drinking with the Prince till Mid-night, and then they sallied out, to go to the place where they meant to Serenade, taking the Prince's Page with them, both to carry their Instruments, and shew them the House. When they were come under the Window, they play'd a while in Consort, till they thought they had awaken'd those of the House, and then the Prince bad *Celadon* give over, and setting his Guittar to answer his Voice, with a passionate Air he sang this Song,

> WHy should my fair Enchantress sleep
> And yet not dream at all of those,
> Whom Love of her in torment keep,
> And hinders from the least repose:
> She has kindled fires in my breast,
> Which keep me still awake,
> And robs her Lover of that rest,
> Which she her self does take.

When he had Sung thus far he heard the Casement open, and one whisper out of it: "Who are you that distrust your own Person and Wit so much, that you make your Court by Musick, to help out the one; and chuse Mid-night for the time to pay your visits in, that Darkness may conceal the defects of the other?"

The Prince (because 'twas a Woman's voice, and because he would willingly have it so) concluded that it was his Mistress, and therefore answered her: *"Those, Madam, who have such Beauty as yours to plead with, ought in their own defence to come in the dark, because in the light, the sight of you would take up so much of their thoughts; that when they have most need of them, to express the greatness of their passion, they'd then be at the greatest loss what to say"*:

"You little think how much you are in the right" (said she) *"for could you see me 'twould spoil your Complementing; for there's nothing so much a bugbear to Wit as an ugly Face"*:

Saying this she clapt to the Window, and nothing which the Prince could afterwards say gain'd any return. He, thinking his Sport over for that Night, looked about for *Celadon*, but no *Celadon* to be found, nor could the Page give any tydings of him: The Prince thought he might be gone home before him, and therefore followed him, in expectation to know how he came to leave him, and to tell him of his Discourse with the Lady.

Here perhaps the Reader may charge *Celadon* with Incivility, in running home before the Prince, when he had promised to keep him company; but let the hasty Censurer have as much patience as the Prince himself, who did not expect to see *Celadon*, till he got to his Lodging, and when he came there, was as far to seek for him as ever; but the next morning, the first who came into his Chamber was *Celadon*, his Complexion was wan, and looked as if he was much out of order: The Prince, who guessed he had been upon an Amour, asked him, what made him look so ill.

"After having begg'd your Highness's Pardon", *said he*, "for my rudeness in leaving you, I'll tell such an accident which befell me since, that your Highness will think a sufficient punishment for it". "While you were Singing, I saw at a little distance something, which, by the whiteness, I guessed to be either a Ghost, or a Woman, and as I am not afraid of either, my Curiosity prompted me see which it was, I walked that way, and found it to be, not a Ghost, but which was worse, a Shee

Devil in a Night-rail,[61] by which I concluded it to be of that Sex which I had most inclination to keep company with at that time of Night; the place too seemed to favour the Temptation, being an old Abby, where there was no body nigh to interrupt us: When I came near her, she broke silence first, and said, *'O Lord, Sir, you have staid very long, I have been waiting for you this hour:'*

"Tho' at first, by her standing there, I thought her Common, yet these words made me take her for some Lover who had made an Assignation; I was resolved to personate him whom the meeting was designed for; and lest she should know my Voice, I answer'd in a low tone, that business hinder'd me, but I would soon make amends for my absence."

Just as he spoke this last word, he runs to the Chamber-door, and having seized a Maid of the House, he hall'd her in, crying out, *"This is the Jilt that play'd me the trick, but I'll be revenged on her"*:

The Maid half dead with fear, could say nothing for her self, but cry'd to the Prince for help; he seeing her gentilely drest, and thinking 'twas his Landlord's Daughter, interposed his Authority, and ordering the Door to be shut, commanded *Celadon* to be calmer, till he enquired into the matter, and asked the Stranger whether she knew what was the reason of his Anger: The Maid desiring that his Highness would hear her, and then judge between them, began thus:

"I perceive by this Gentleman's Anger, that he has been grossly abused; that I have been in some sort the cause, I am sorry; but to shew you I am a very innocent one, I'll give you a relation of some passages of my life, which though publickly known, yet never should have been told you by me, were it not such an important account as this, the allaying this Gentleman's rage against me, and the hindering him from noising any thing abroad, which might be to the prejudice of my Reputation:"

"My Father is a Country Gentleman, descended from a good Family, but his Ancestors were so improvident, as to spend most of their Estate, and leave him but a small remainder to maintain a great many Children: I am the youngest of all, the Favourite both of Father and Mother, whose greatest care has been to Match me so, that they may live to see me happy. I had choice enough; for these three or four years I have had little rest from Suitors, who from all parts of the Country sollicited me: My Fortune, I believe, they did not court me for, because I saw several who had far greater were neglected; People flatter'd me indeed with the title of a Beauty, and Fame, who is most commonly a great Lyar, did lift my Name among her wonders; whether she was in the wrong or no, I could wish she were, for it has put me to more trouble than a good Face is worth, to bear with the several impertinencies of my Country Servants; though to have seen their several humours would have been as good as a Comedy to me, had I been meerly a Spectator, but I lost the pleasure because I was an Actress in it my self: Every one of them had a particular behaviour, yet every one something of the *Harlequin* in it; and their Courtship was different, according to their diversity of humours: "

"One had Confidence, and thought that would gain me, and he'd be the most troublesome, because he'd touzé[62] me and hale me about, and I had much ado to defend my self from his rudeness; him I avoided as I would the Devil. "

"Another would think to gain me by his over-civility, and he'd come a great way just to ask me how I did, and how my Father and Mother did, ask me what a Clock it was, and what time of the Moon, and where I was at Church last *Sunday*; and after some such wise discourse, he'd take a kiss and be gone; he was my Chip in Porridge,[63] I neither shunned his Company, nor cared for it. "

"A third, pufft up with the good success of having gotten his Father's Maid, or Tenant's Daughter with Child, believed the same Methods would conquer me, and therefore thought to entertain me with immodest discourse; my Vertue made me deaf to all he could say, and for my Reputation sake I avoided him. "

"Then a widower came, a Cousen, addressed to me, desiring to be nearer a-kin, and thought to touch my heart, but indeavoured it after so rude a manner, as if he forgot that 'twas a Maid, not a Widow, he was Courting: But it appeared, for all his long practising Merchandise, that he did not know how to Purchase, for all that he had in the World could not buy my consent to give him mine."

"A fifth was opinionative of his rustick valour, and he'd aim at conquering his Mistress the same way as Knights Errant did of old, by quarrelling and beating every one he came near: But I thought such an over-boyling Courage, which would still expose me to fears for him, was fitter for a Bravo,[64] than a Husband."

"The sixth was my true Country Courtier, who was all innocence; he had scarce Courage enough to keep him from swooning, when he came into my Company, unless his Spirits had been raised before-hand, by a dram of the Bottle, or a belly full of strong drink; then he'd say, his Mother sent him to ask me whether I'd have him; and tell me a long story of his Ground, his Dairy, and his Cattle; I despised this Milksop, and thought it a hard bargain to give myself in subjection to the chief Beast, only to be mistress of the rest."

"This was my condition, when a young Gentleman, a Stranger, came down into our Country to some Friends he had there; and no sooner saw me, than he encreased the number of my Captives, and professed himself my Servant, but when he first told it me, 'twas with all the Rhetorick which an ingenious passion could invent, his Eyes, his Actions, and every gesture so gracefully seconded his Story, that the Lover's part, which the others acted so ridiculously, became him so well, as if he were only made for Love. When he paid a visit, if any of the rest chanced to come at the same time, the Breeding which he brought from *Dublin,* elevated him so far above them, in his Discourse, his Carriage, and all he did, that they did look like our wild *Irish* to him; but when alone he talked to me of Love, the Musick of his tongue was so enchanting, I could have staid and listen'd for ever to him."

"Sir, I will say no more in his commendation, for methinks Lovers are so much a part of our selves, that their praises look fulsome where they come from one another, I will only tell your Highness that we were but too happy in one another, till Fortune, who is never constantly kind, contrived a way to part us asunder: But why should we curse our ill Fortune, or lay the fault on the Devil, when any mischance does befall us? Whereas poor *Beelzebub* is wrong'd, for he could not do us half the mischiefs we receive, unless we helped him against one another, and of all people I think the Envious are his principal Agents, of which this is a remarkable instance":

"There lived in the same House with him, one *Capella*, a stale Maid, of a good Family, but a decayed Fortune, and she, it seems, hearing of our Amour, envied the happiness of it: I can't say 'twas out of any violent Love to him, for her being pretty far advanced in years, and sickly besides, do make me think her Loving time was past, at least I'm sure it should have been, for her grey Hairs, her Dwarfishness, her Sickliness, her Pale Ill-favoured Face, and her want of a Fortune to gild all these Imperfections, might have hindered her from thinking of Marriage, if she had any Wit to consider them; but she will repent the want of it, when the foolish desire of Intriguing in her old Age, has rendered her ridiculous to all the Gentlemen, and after wasting her Youth in Pride and Disdain of those that more than deserved her, make her take up at last, for want of a better, with a Ploughman, a Groom, or a Footman. I fear your Highness will think this a very illnatur'd Character, but I will beg you to consider, that it proceeds from her own deserts, and the resentment an injured Love does usually raise in our Breasts, against those who are the chief causes of our unhappiness; as certainly she was of mine, for the Nets she often, and in vain, spread for others, were now laid for him: And because she thought the Love of me diverted him; after having with Jeers and Perswasions, Scorn and Flattery, Anger and Kindness, and all the different ways she could think on, in vain attempted to shake his Constancy; she was resolved to make me lose him, though she lost him her self by it; and getting some of her Relations to represent me to his, as disadvantageously as they could, they (lest he should loiter away his Youth in Love, and not pursue that Preferment to which his Genius was likely to raise him) called him up to *Dublin.*"

"I, partly to hush the discourse which her Malice had raised of us, about the Countrey, partly, because it made me melancholly, to see those deserted Shades,⁶⁵ where I had formerly been so happy, quitted that place, and chose my Aunt's House, where your Highness is now, for my retirement. He came to Town, *incognito*, to see me, and for fear some of his Friends should hear of it, our meetings were always in private. "

"An Abbey hard by (being solitary and free from any company that might disturb us) we pitched upon our last nights Assignation: I was there first, and this Gentleman coming by, I mistook him for the other: He'll own himself that he began to be too familiar, and lest he should offer me violence at that time of night, when no body was near to help me, I was driven to this shift to get rid of him: I saw which way his nature inclined him, and thence concluded there was no way to deliver my self, but by putting him in hopes of some better intrigue; I therefore told him, I would not detain him from my Mistresses's Embraces, who had been waiting for him this long while (pretending I mistook him for some other Gentleman) and so drew him from thence, designing at the first House I saw any up, to pretend she was there and so leave him: I durst not come home with him, lest the vexation of finding himself deceiv'd, should make him raise the House, and to come home with an Officer at that time of Night, would have ruined me in my Aunt's good opinion. "

"It fell out as well as I could wish, for an Ale-house was open, and desiring him to go and enquire for her there, I bad him good night, and came home as fast as my fear could carry me: What became of him after I know not, only desire that he would impute it to his own Curiosity, if he has suffered; and that both your Highness and he will be so honourable, as to keep what I have related from others Ears, as strictly as I would have kept it from yours, had I not been constrained to reveal it in justification of mine Honour."

The Prince, who had listened with delight to the Love-story, it jumping so well with the humour he was then in, told the young Gentlewoman, that he had a great respect for her, as she was a Gentlewoman, and so near a Relation of his Landladies, but more, as she was Beautiful, Vertuous, and a Lover, and wished her a great deal of Success.

Celadon begg'd a thousand pardons for the rudeness his Ignorance had betray'd him to; and that she might be more inclined to pardon him, he desired her to stay, and hear the unlucky adventure he had after she left him. The Prince desired her to seat her self, and *Celadon* with half a smile, and a blush together, thus continued his Story.

"You may remember, Madam, that I promised you to make amends for my long stay, and went about to be as good as my word, had not your Vertue and Cunning restrained me more than my own: And tho' I have all along said that no Woman could resist Opportunity and Importunity, yet now I renounce my Error, and could my self become a Proselyte to Chastity, were I so happy as the Gentleman you waited for, I mean, in having so Fair, so Vertuous a Mistress, to regulate my wandering desires, and confine them to her self; as it is, your example, and last nights trick put upon me, have half Converted me: I will own to you, that I did really think that you had mistaken me for another; I was big with hopes of the Bliss you promised to conduct me to; and 'twas either your wisdom, or good luck, not to go into the light with me; I saw indeed so much of you, as to know you again by your Cloaths; but had I seen that alluring Face, your feigned Mistress had not served your turn; I did not, because I avoided your seeing mine, for fear you should discover me to be the wrong Person:

"For the same reason, I was loath to ask your Mistress's Name, and chose rather to enquire for her at a venture, concluding, that if I once came into her Company, the fear of my discovering her Amour would over-awe her, and make her as kind to me, as if I were the Spark that she waited for: Besides, the heat of my Inclination pushed me forward at a venture, whether I succeeded or no:

"I went therefore into the House, and asked a Boy at the Bar, whether there was ever a Gentlewoman there who expected me: The Boy asked me what her Name was: *"What's that to you"* said I? *"Is there ever a Gentlewoman in the House?"* The Boy, who understood his Trade, guessed what I meant; shewed me a Room, and sent in a Woman to me":

"Her colour was very good, for I believe she was Painted, her Look was brisk, and her Garb gentile enough; for my Garb being pretty rich, they thought to make a good Prize of me, and therefore sent me, I suppose, the choicest Girl in the House. I took her to be the distressed Wife of some old Man, who had married her to make her his Nurse, and therefore told her it belong'd to my Profession to help the distressed."

"She told me she thought, by my Tone and Whiskers that I was an Out-landish[66] Man; asked me how long I had been in Town, and whether I was a meer stranger to that place; pretending as if she was afraid of my coming to the knowledge of whose Wife she was. I told her I was an *English-man,* had been beyond Sea several years; that I came to Town but two or three days ago, with the Prince's Troops, and should suddenly be marching to *Limerick,* and that therefore she should make the better use of me while I staid, and never fear a discovery afterwards; by this she guessed I should never be able to find the House again; and that embolden'd them to deal as they did with me; she seemed to be so cautious, out of a fear of her Honour; when therefore she had gotten as much knowledge of my being a Stranger, as satisfied her fears, she began to be more familiar with me, and, out of a particular piece of kindness, would needs send out for a Bottle of Sack for me, saying, she would drink a health to the good man at home; we both laughed at the conceit; I, how little he thought of his Horns,[67] and she to think how little I suspected the Trick she was going to play me":

"The Wine she would needs drink mull'd, and, ordering it herself, she infused either Opiate, or some such Soporiferous draught; we had no sooner drank it off, than she consented to go to Bed, saying, that her Husband was out of Town, and the House belonging to a Friend of hers, no body was likely to trouble our pleasures: Because I suspected nothing, I never minded how little she drank; and you know, Madam, we usually indulge Women their liberty in drinking, therefore very likely she drank less, and so it might have less operation upon her; it worked so on me, that I did not wake till late in the morning, and when I first opened my Eyes, I found my self in the innermost part of the Abby, which I saw you at last Night;"

"I was laid on a Tombstone, by the side of a great Marble Statue (the Effigies of some Great Person formerly buried there) I wonder'd to find that my Bed and Bedfellow had both suffered such a Niobetick[68] alteration, that they who were so soft and warm last Night, were become so hard and cold by Morning; but I wonder'd more at my self, when I found no Cloaths, but an old *Franciscan* Habit on me, I began to think of *Plato's* transmigration, and that I had died an Officer, and for my lewdness in my former body, was doom'd now to be an abstinent *Franciscan*: But I had not much time to think, for by this time, a zealous Neighbour that had seen me asleep, thought he would catch a Frier napping, and brought a constable for me; the Man of Authority order'd me immediately to appear before a Justice of the Peace."

"I was conducted in State through the Streets, at the head of a Party, more numerous than your Highness's body of Souldiers; they huzza'd all the way, as if the King were going by; and methought I went in great Pomp, only my Triumph was after the *Roman* fashion, with the Lictor[69] behind me, who every now and then threat'ned me with Bridewell, the Stocks, and the Gibbet: In this manner I marched near half a mile to the Justice's, barefooted all the way, which I think of it self was sufficient pennance for my last nights Debauch":

"The Justice asked me a great many impertinent questions; as how I durst appear there in that Habit? and why I did not go after the *French* to *Limerick?* I saw it best to confess what I was, and told him all the latter part of my adventure, how that the People of the House knowing, by my own confession, that I was a Stranger, and not likely to find the House again, had robb'd me of all my Cloaths at Mid-night, and left me there in an old Habit, which some poor Holy Brother had formerly given them as the return of a kindness: The Justice would not believe but this was a Jesuitical evasion of mine, and therefore bad me, if I was a Souldier, send for some body that I was acquainted with;

I named two or three Officers of my Acquaintance, and the Justice sent one for them, they were found in a Tavern with a great deal of other Company, and the fellow delivering his Message publickly, they all came to see the Novice in his Habit; their Testimony released me, and I was fain to borrow some Cloaths to go home in, having lost a very good Suit of my own, and most part of the ready Money I have in the World, and have got nothing for it, but the name of *Celadon* the *Franciscan*, which will stick by me as long as I live":

"Your Highness may see now the cause of my paleness, is the potion I drank, and the cold Lodging I had, which if it had not happen'd at such a hot time of the year, would have made me dye in a more Religious Habit than ever I lived in. You, Madam, if you have any such thing as pity in you, will excuse me, and think that the shame, the loss, and the cold I suffered might be sufficient cause to make me angry with you, whilst I thought you one of the Accomplices."

The fair Stranger, with a pitying smile, told him, That she was sorry he had suffered so much by her means, and said, that to shew she did no way consent to it, she would send one who should shew him the House; and if he would carry a Constable with him, he might recover all his things again.

The Prince, who had laughed till he was weary, bad *Celadon* call up the Centry, him he sent for a File of Musqueteers, and desiring the beautiful Stranger to send a Guide with them to the House, sent *Celadon* with them.

The young Gentlewoman, bidding the Prince good morrow, went to her Uncle and Aunt to give them some share of the Laughter, and ordering one of the Servants to go with the Souldiers to the House, there *Celadon* found his last nights Mistress, and having recovered his Cloaths and his Watch, he sent for the same Constable, who had conducted him so carefully to the Justice's, and leaving his Mistress, and her fellow Nuns to the publick Justice, he came back to the Prince very well satisfied that he had come off so well, and brought his experience so cheap.

Though the oddness of *Celadon*'s adventure did for some time employ the Prince's mind, yet at last, by a long chain of thought, he returned to the accustomed Subject his Mistress: For as the *Jack of the Lanthorn* is said to lead the benighted Country-man about, and makes him tread many a weary step in fruitless rounds, yet leaves him near the same place where it found him at first; so Love's deluding fire, after enticing the blinded mind through many restless thoughts, brings it about again to its beloved Idea, that enchanting circle it can never leave; 'twas this bewitching Passion which brought our Prince from *Celadon*'s adventure to the fair Strangers, and from hers to his own; and when he call'd to mind the Story of her Lover, and his success over her heart, he pleaded himself with hopes of the like Fortune in his own Amour, and thought it very probable, that a Prince, who had several advantages over one of a private Fortune, might expect the same success, and not fear the like disappointment, since he had no power to over-awe, or check his Love, or Relations to controul it.

Finding a great deal of diversion in his melancholly entertainment, he resolved on a walk, as well to take the Air, as to prevent the engaging himself in any Company, which might come to seek him at his Lodgings; when he had walked about half a mile, he found himself on top of a Hill, whence having looked a while on the adjacent Town, and with a curious Eye searched out that part of it, which his admired Beauty made happy with her presence, he laid him down under the shade of two or three large Trees, whose spreading Boughs nature had woven so close together, that neither the heat of the Sun, nor storm of the fiercest Wind could violate the pleasant shade, which was made as a general defence, no less against the scorching of the one, than the nipping of the other; they seemed to have been the first planted there, for the shelter of those who came thither to drink; for just by there bubbled up a clear and plentiful Spring, of which, from an ancient *Irish* Chronicle, let me give you this Story. *Cluaneesha*, the only child of *Macbuain*, King of *Munster*, was accused of having been too familiar with one of her Father's Courtiers; the Fact was attested upon oath by two Gentlemen that awaited on the King's Person, and to confirm it, the Princess her self had such a swelling in her, that few doubted but their Witness was true, and would soon be proved by her being brought to Bed: Her Father, being old and sickly, was desired, for the prevention of Civil Wars after his Death, to nominate a Successour: The people shewed their unanimous consent to confer the Crown on her Uncle, because they would not have a Strumpet for their Sovereign; so the old King was perswaded to proclaim his Brother Heir Apparent, and condemn his Daughter to a Cloister: The Courtier fled beyond Sea, and went a Pilgrimage to the Saint at *Posnanie*; the very night that he arrived there, one appeared to the Mother Abbess, in the form of a Nun glorified, and told her, that she was *Edith*, Daughter formerly to King ―――― but now in happiness; that she loved Chastity and innocence while she was on Earth, and therefore defended it still; that she was constrained to leave the seat of Bliss to protect Vertue, injured in the Person of *Cluaneesha*; that the persons who swore against her were suborn'd; that the swelling of her Belly was but a Disease; and that if she and the witnesses would go and drink of a Well, which sprung out of a Hill near *Clonmell*, there she would convince all the Spectators, that what she now told her was true: The Abbess told this the next day to the King's Confessor, and he told it the King; the King ordered one who was Confessor to the two Witnesses, to enjoin them, for their next pennance, to drink no other Liquor, but the Water of this Well, for a Week together; they obey'd him, but it was their last, for it made them swell as if they were poisoned; in the mean time the Mother Abbess came down thither with her Royal Novice.

She charged them with the Perjury, and they confessed publickly, that the King's brother, taking the advantage of that swelling, which he thought was but a Tympany, suborned them to swear against her Chastity, expecting that either it would kill her, or at least it might deceive the People so long till the King was dead, and he in possession of the Crown: A certain Citizen of *Clonmell*, who came among the rest to see them dying, and heard the Confession, admiring the strange virtue of the Water, went immediately home to his Wife, and telling her that he was suspicious of her Honesty, and desired that, to satisfie his Jealousie, she would drink a draught of Water, and wish it might be her last, if she were unfaithful: She not having yet heard of the others punishment, and willing to clear her self, drank of it as he desired, but swell'd with it as the others did, and dyed soon after in great torment.

When the Well had grown famous by the exemplary deaths of the Perjured Witnesses, and the Adulterate Citizen, the Princess declared she would drink of it too; and that the clearing of her self might be as publick as her accusation was, she sent up to the King, who was then at *Cork*, to desire that her Uncle himself might be present when she drank, to witness her innocence; he excused himself, and would not go, but a great many of the Court coming thither to see the Princess clear her self, she went in solemn Procession barefoot, from the City to the Well; and taking up a glass full of the Water, she protested her Innocence, and using the same imprecation with the others, if she did not speak the truth, drank it off; but instead of working the same effect on her, it in a little time cured her of the Disease she had, recovered her Health, and with it brought her so much Beauty, that all the neighbouring Princes were Rivals for her:

She had design'd to build a Nunnery by that Well, but her Father dying left her the cares of a Crown, which diverted her from it: But the Well was long after reverenced, and for the quality it had of discovering Unchastity, it was much resorted to; for the Inhabitants of *Ireland* (how barbarous soever the partial Chronicles of other Nations report'em) were too nice in Amour to take a polluted Wife to their Bed, as long as this Well would shew them which was a chast one; but the wickedness of after-times grew too guilty to bear with such Tryals; thence by disuse this Well lost its Fame, and perhaps its Vertue.

And now I will no longer tell such Tales, but leave the uncertain Lover to take his Lot as it comes.

Pretty near this Well the Prince lay down, and being pleased with the murmuring of its Stream running down a descent of the Hill, that, and his want of Sleep the night before, tempted him to take it now; *Morpheus* was ready at his call, and waving his Leaden Rod over him, lull'd all his Senses, till a greater power than he rescued him from sleep, to Charm him in a more prevailing manner; for as he waked he heard one hemm, and found it was in order to Sing, for presently the unknown, with a ravishing Air, began this Song.

> Yield, Souldier, yield, give up your Sword,
> And don't rebel in vain,
> Yield on all conquering Beauty's word,
> And take what quarter she'll afford,
> And you shall wear the lighter Chain.
>
> Why do you put such trust in Art?
> In vain, fond Wretch, you Arm,
> And think Steel proof 'gainst Beauty's dart,
> Which will, like light'ning, pierce your Heart,
> yet do your Coat of Mail no harm.

The excellency of the Voice, and the suitableness of the Sence to his own condition, made him lye still to hearken to her that Sung it, and listening very attentively, he over-heard another Voice, which breaking silence began thus.

"I thank you, dear *Marinda*, for the Song, I like the Tune you have put to it, and either that, and the sweetness of your Voice, do make me partial, or else the Song is very good: I like the Authority it carries with it, for I am usually well pleased when I hear those Songs, which attribute so much power to our Sex; but prethee tell me, why is a Souldier the aim of it? when I have heard you say, that a Souldier should be your last choice, because they are always abroad, and therefore very seldom enjoy'd after Marriage, and while they are Suitors their Pride makes them the most troublesome, and the most inconstant of any; when they pay a visit, if there be a Glass in the Room, they look more on themselves, than on her they came to see, and as often as they look on their Scarf and Feather, their Vanity puffs them up so, that if we yield not immediately, they Swear and Curse, and so fall off, taking it as an unpardonable affront that we don't admire them at first sight; and when they are beloved, their Self-conceit makes them place it to the account of their own Merits, and so they value our Love the less, because they think it their due; nay, and are not contented with a single Conquest, be it ever so fine a one, and as they do not fight for Malice, so neither do they court for Love, but out of the pure vain-glory of Conquering; and take as much Pride in having abundance of Mistresses, as abundance of Souldiers to follow them."

"You observe right" (*said she who was called* Marinda) "I'le grant to you, that for these considerations, they are both the worst of Servants, and worst of her Husbands, and yet in a brave Souldier there is something so Noble, I mean in his not fearing dangers, and his patient endurance of all manner of hardships, that were it not for the aforemention'd inconveniencies of Absence, Pride, and Inconstancy, I should have a greater value for such a one, than ever I yet had for any other Employment":

"Nay, now *Marinda*" (*reply'd the other*) "you make good the Character which our Sex bears among the Men, of being inconstant as the Wind; for 'twas but two or three days ago you were of a clear contrary Opinion, and you knew the same qualities of Courage and Hardiness to be then in a Souldier which you do now, and therefore they are no just reasons why you should alter your mind; they make some shew of being Arguments indeed, but I have observed that Wits, when they alter their Opinions, whether it be in point of Religion, Allegiance, or any thing else, never want something to say in their own defence":

"Well, since you are so desirous" (*said* Marinda) "to know the cause of this alteration of humour in me, I'll tell it you; though in doing so, I rather follow the dictates of Friendship than Discretion, and prove kinder to you than to my self, in telling you that which I am almost ashamed to think of.

"You know that about three or four days ago a Party of Foreigners made their entrance into this Town, with the prince of S ——— g at the head of them, Curiosity made me open my Window to see them pass by, either the desire of looking about him, or the pride of being gazed at, made the Prince ride slower by that place than ordinary, and he had his design, for I looked as stedfastly on him, as if he had been the only Pageant there; and tho', without doubt, there were several Officers very brave and fine; yet the seeing him first had so prejudiced me in favour of him, that I could not think the rest worth the looking on; all the rest of that day I could not forbear thinking of him, fancying I saw with what a Grace he sat his Horse, how stately he look'd, so far beyond the rest of his Souldiers, as if nature, as well as Fortune, had marked him out for a Prince and distinguished him from the rest, as much by his person, as by his power; and as the thoughts of the day have an effect upon those at night, so I believe these were the cause of my being disturbed in my Bed with this Dream.

"The Prince, methought, in my absence, had hidden himself in my Bed-chamber, and, when I came in, started out upon me: He had on one side of him a little wing'd Archer, who bent his Bow, and aimed at me several times; but just by me there started up a great Gigantick form, with no other Arms but a Shield, and he, methought, still interposed that, and with it kept off the Arrows of the other; at length, methought, the Prince spoke something which tempted my Defender over to his side, and left me to the Mercy of the young Archer, who shot me through and through; and at the same instant the Prince came and catched me in his Arms, and told me I was his Prisoner, at which, methought, I swooned away with a pleasing pain, and at the fright of it I awaked."

"People say dreams are significant, if they are, tell me what you think is the meaning of this?"

"Why truly," (*said the other*) "any one who should hear you tell this, might guess, without any great skill in Fortune telling, that you are in Love":

"If" (*said* Marinda) "I did think a little the day before upon the Prince, which might have been the cause (*as you say*) of this Dream, yet those thoughts were too slightly grounded to be of any long continuance, and I was in hopes in a day or two to have clearly rooted them out; and the next Afternoon one of my Acquaintance came to desire my Company to a Ball, I was ready enough to accept of the proffer, because I imagined that the

Musick and the Company would cure me of my thoughtfulness; but (as my ill Fate would have it) it was clear contrary; for whom should I meet at the Ball but the Prince; you were there, and saw how I was clearly put out of my Dance, with the confusion his presence put me in:

"He sate down with me, and made me some few Compliments, which tho', perhaps, were coveted by some of the Company, yet had those Ladies seen my inside, as well as they did my outside, they would rather have pitied, than envied me; 'twas he that sung under my Window last night, and though you mistook him for your Servant, yet I knew his deluding Voice too well: His words were so pathetical, and the Tune so moving, that though he had skill enough at the Guittar, which he plaid on, yet that kept not time with his Voice truer than my Pulse and Heart did."

"Have a care *Marinda*" (*said the other*) "that you do not engage too far with one who is so much above you; 'tis not safe Intriguing with Persons of his Quality; Inferior Lovers may be jested with as long as we please, and thrown off at will, but such as he seldom leave us without carrying away our Vertue, or at least our Reputation: And you will too late curse your own Charms when they have exposed you to be ruined (like a young Conjurer) by raising a Spirit which you are not able to lay."

"I fear" (*reply'd* Marinda) "he has spy'd something in my behaviour that (he fancied) favoured him, as Mens conceitedness makes them too apt to discover such things; I am sorry for it, if I did discover any weakness in my self, that should encourage him to such an attempt: I am sure my Tongue never dropt the least word in his favour; and if my tell-tale Eyes, or my Countenance has betray'd me, I'll disfigure this Countenance, and tear out these Eyes, rather than they shall invite, or assist any enterprize, to the prejudice of my Vertue."

Now though I have told the Reader the discourse these Ladies had in private, yet let him not expect that I shall tell him the Prince's thoughts upon it; that I should not be able to do, though I had been in his heart, for they were so different, that he scarce knew what to make of them himself: He certainly had need of a great presence of mind, to resolve upon such a sudden what to do, whether to discover himself, or no: If he did, he saw some probability that the Lady might be kinder, when she knew that he had heard her confessing a Love for him; if he did not interrupt them, he thought he might hear more; but while he was in this irresolution he chanced to Sneeze, at which the Ladies arose from the seat which they were on by the Well, and walked away, very likely because they found somebody was nearer than they had imagined, and were afraid of being overheard in their discourse:

The Prince lay a while musing on what he had heard, and then went home; he related it all to *Celadon*, and asked his advice what use he should make of it: *Celadon* told him it was not the safest way to extort a confession of love from her, by letting her know he had over-heard her, because that might make her angry at his hearkening, and such a discovery might be too violent for a Maiden Modesty, and so nice a one as hers seemed to be; he desired him rather to continue his Addresses, and so bring her by degrees to a voluntary submission; that this was the more natural and the surer way; that twice or thrice more being in her Company would ensure his Conquest over her; and what need was there to hazard her displeasure, by forcing her to confess she loved him, when he was well enough satisfied of it already?

The Prince consented to this, and contrived this way to see her; he knew the Town was so full of Souldiers, that every House had some of them in it, he thought hers quartered some Officers, and enquiring out who they were, he told *Celadon* that he would go and see them at their Lodgings:

That Evening they went together to the House, and a Maid shewing them into the Parlour, they found there *Marinda* and two Strangers, one of which the Prince knew to be the same he had seen at the Well with her; they would have left the Room when they saw the Prince come in, but he was too well skill'd in War to let a weak Enemy retreat, he had not fought her out to let her go so easily; he was thinking of some shift to put off the Officers, whom the Maid was gone to call, when to his great satisfaction she brought him word, they were not at home: He said, that having so pleasing Company, he could very well stay till they came in, and sitting down, he made a sign to *Celadon* to entertain the Strangers, to give him the greater freedom with *Marinda*; and that he had not long, for the Mother came in: Then she (as old Women usually do) took up most of the talk her self, till the Prince, tired with it, took his leave: As they walked home, *Celadon* asked the Prince what he thought of *Marinda*.

"I take her", (*said the Prince*) "to be the most perfect Innocence that ever was since the fall of *Eve*: Her words are so Witty, and yet so modest, her humour so nicely Vertuous, and yet so Civil, that I account the Country Ignorance which is in her, to be beyond all the breeding in the World."

"I told her that I made an advantagious exchange in getting her Company, by their not being within whom I came to see; she said, she was not of the same opinion, since if Men in general were as good Company as I, she must needs blame the unkindness of Nature, which had made her of so unsociable a Sex, that she was neither Wit enough to converse with Men, nor would the Rules of vertue give a Maid that liberty, if she were otherwise qualified for it: I told her that all who knew her but so much as I did, must needs contradict her, in that nature had given her Wit as well as Beauty; that the one was made to delight the Ears of Men, the other their Eyes; and as without always closetting her self up, she could not bar us from the last, so neither, without great injustice, could she deprive us of the one half of our happiness, by tying her self up to an obstinate silence, meerly to deprive us of the other."

"She smiled, and said, she had not power enough over her self to observe that silence which a Maid ought; but that since men, by their insinuating discourse, drew words from her which she should keep in, she would shun the Company of that deluding Sex, and so keep her self from yielding so much to them, by not coming within reach of the temptation: She blushed as she spoke these words, and I might have gained ground mightily on her yielding heart, if the old Gentlewoman had not unfortunately come in to her rescue."

The Prince pleased himself much with the thoughts of his Conquest, but he knew not what a stubborn Enemy Vertue is, and how difficult it would be for him to take any advantage over a Heart, which that maintain'd against him.

Having found so little resistance at his first visit, he believed *Celadon*'s observation was true, that two or three more would win her; he went often, under pretence of seeing the officers, and sometimes met with them, but never with *Marinda*; once or twice the Servants said she was abroad, but the last time he enquired for her, they said she was sick; he fancied that she had ordered the Servants to deny her, and therefore judged the readiest way to see her would be by his former Stratagem, a Ball; and that he might not be expected there, he gave out the Evening before, that he was going for *Dublin* the next day to get Orders from the King: He rode through the Town that Morning, and her House being in the way, he called at the Door, and asked to speak with one of the Officers that lodged there, but to the intent that she might take notice where he was going: When he was out of sight of the Town, he rode back again to his Lodgings another way, keeping close, that nobody might know of his return; and when he thought the Ball was at the highest, he and *Celadon* went there together; the place where they Danced was the same where the first Ball was, the Company almost the same, only that it wanted the Beautiful *Marinda*, but in wanting her it wanted all, nothing there was worthy to entertain our Prince, therefore he called to *Celadon* to go with him home; but *Celadon* was of another mind, he was not so nice in his choice, to retire himself from such variety of good Company, meerly for the absence of one; he was very little pleased with the capriciousness of the Prince's humour, and would have willingly staid behind, if he had thought it would not disoblige him:

But the Prince being desirous to go, they took leave of the Company, and were going out together, when, at the Door, they were met by a couple of Ladies in a strange *Spanish* dress; and their Faces, after the mode of that Nation, had long Vails over them: *Celadon* bobb'd the Prince, and desired him to come back to see what Masks those were, telling him, that under them he might chance to find *Marinda*; the Prince was in hopes of it too, and made up to them, but found himself deceived; for speaking to one of them in *French*, she seemed not to understand him, but whispered to the other, and she spoke to him in *Spanish*, asking him whether he was not the Prince of S ——— g, Commander of the Forces now in Town? The Prince answer'd her that he was; but desired her if she could speak any other language to do it, for he understood very little of that.

"I speak, Sir," (*said she*) "a little *English*, and if your Highness can understand me better in that, I shall beg the honour of a hearing from you, for I do not know but it may lye in your Highness power to do me a great kindness":

"What is that kindness, pretty Petitioner" (*said* Celadon) "for all your excellent counterfeiting (Madam) I fancy you are two of this Town, that pretend some sober business with us now, and design to laugh at us when ye are gone, for being so little curious, as to see nothing of a Lady but her dress."

"That you may not think" (*said the other Lady in broken* English) "that we are not of this Countrey, we'll dance you a Sarabrand after the *Spanish* way, and if that will not convince you, I can shew you so ugly a Face, that mine shall be the last Veil you shall ever desire to look under":

"Let us have the Dance" (*said* Celadon) "and if your Air and Meen be as becoming as your Shape, I shall venture to look in your Faces, for all your threatening."

The Company left off Dancing to look at these two, whose dress seem'd so extraordinary, and the Prince, who had a mind to see them Dance, ordered the Musick to play such a Tune as pleased them best, and they with their Castinets acquitted themselves very gracefully, and came off with the commendation of all the Company: Their Shapes and Carriage being very near alike, *Celadon* did not know which to like best of them; he told them that now he must desire to see their Faces, that the handsomest might take him all to her self, and free him from the double Captivity he now lay under, of being a Slave to them both; but one of them told him they could not grant it, for she had a boon to the Prince, in the begging of which she must open such private passages of her Life, as would make her ashamed to be seen by the Man that knew them; but if it e're lay in the Prince's power to grant her it, then she would turn *English* Woman, and throw off her Veil.

The Prince said that was a very plausible excuse, and desired *Celadon* to urge the Strangers no more, and turning to them, told them, that whomsoever that Story concerned, he desired she would tell him, and he would, according to her directions, serve her to the utmost of his power.

Both the Strangers gave him a very low Courtesie, in token of their thankfulness; and one of them desiring the patience of his Highness, and the rest of the Company, seating her self in the midst of them who had left their dancing to listen to her, she began thus,

The Story of Faniaca

"PErhaps this Company, and more particularly that part of it which is of my own Sex, may censure this freedom in me, and think it too much openness in a Maid, to discover things of such privacy in a publick audience, which the rest of Womankind make their Closet secrets; but my *Spanish* Mistress, upon this very occasion, told me a Story of a *Spartan* Boy, who having stolen a young Fox, and hidden him under his Gown, rather than be discovered, kept him there till he tore out his Bowels: So it is with the *English* Ladies, if once Love enters into their Breasts, though, like that Fox, it prey upon their Hearts, yet out of Modesty they keep it secret; and though the closer it is hid, it gnaws the fiercer, yet, like the poor proud Boy, they hug it to 'em, and conceal it till it ruins them: But the *Spaniards,* and those of my Country, who are in a hotter Clime, tye not themselves up to such cold, such rigid Rules of Honour: Your Love, like your Winter Sun, is so clouded, that those he should shine on are never the better for him; ours is so hot and predominant, that there is nothing can cover him: Now you your selves cannot give a good reason for this nice piece of Modesty, which allows you to take a fancy to a fine Dog, a fine Horse, or anything else that is handsome, only Man, which is the stateliest, gayest Creature of all, you must not own a regard for:

"Sure this Tyrannical custom was founded at first by some old decrepid Matrons, that were past the enjoyment of Love themselves; for Nature, that has allowed you the publick freedom of all other pleasures of life, would never consent to disgrace this sweetest of all: Whence comes it then, that tho' most of you are fond of it, yet you manage it so secretly, as if it were Treason to our Sex to own it? While I am in *England* I should dissemble, like the *English*; but pardon me for once, if I break this general rule, in searching for a Lover, whom I can never find, but by discovering my self wherever I come, that some of those who hear me, may chance to bring the same story to his Ears, that so he may find me again."

"My Name is *Faniaca*, my Father was a *Brachman*,[72] an *Indian* Priest in the Province of *Antis*, which Countrey having never been conquered by the *Incas*, kept up the ancient Barbarity, not being Civilized by their Laws, as those Nations were, who had yielded to their Government: And whereas they with one consent worshipped the Sun, we of Antis had several Deities, the two chief of which were the Tyger, and a large Serpent, which we called *Amaru*: To these it was our custom to sacrifice Human Blood; they commonly fed on nothing else but Captives, and if we had no Captives, we were forced to find them the same sort of Food from among our selves: But we rarely found any such want, for there being an irreconcileable Enmity, first between us and the *Incas*, and then with those Indians who took part with the *Spaniards*, we had so frequent Engagements, they to extend their Dominions, and we to defend our own, that scarce a day happened, but brought us in some new Prisoners; for the *Spaniards* had a great Colony at Cozco, and from thence they every now and then sent Parties far into our Countrey to take Booties, and make discoveries of the Land, in order to a farther Conquest":

"These Parties were commonly made up of *Indians* with *Spaniards* to head them, because they would willingly spare their own Nation, and Conquer ours at the Natives expence. These *Spaniards* still encroached farther on us, till they had driven us over the *Madalena*, that great River, being very deep, of a strong swift Current, and at that place about a League broad, made it seem as if our differences were now at an end, Nature it self having divided us: On each side of the River there was a considerable Town, of which, the one was possessed by their Party, the other by ours; and though sometimes our Fishermen would meet by chance and kill, or take one another, yet we never gave one another a troublesome visit on shore, by reason that our Canoes were not big enough to transport Men in so-great numbers, as to dare to Land; and it being about 300 Leagues down the Sea, we never had seen, or could imagine any which should hold above ten or twelve men at most; for our Canoes were made all of a piece, and how to put different Planks together, as Ship-Carpenters do, was an Art wholly unknown to us":

"Some of the *Spaniards* had taught our Enemies this, and they privately built a great many large Flat-bottoms, which the Governour of their Town fill'd with *Indians*, and sent a few of his own Countrey-men with them; these Forces he sent over about Mid-night, with orders to Land at our Town, kill all the Men, and sending back the Boats, to keep the Town till he Landed an Army sufficient to fight his way farther into the Country."

"In this Town my Father lived, and was Priest to the Tiger and an *Amanu*, which were accounted the largest of any thereabouts, and therefore were worshipped the most, and had their Adorers to bring them presents from all parts."

"Those *Indians* who took the *Spaniards* part, were always very inveterate against us, because the *Incas* made both their Government and Religion different from ours; as soon therefore as they entered the Town they kill'd all, without any distinction either of Sex or Age; I was awakened out of my sleep with a dreadful cry, such as you may imagine that of a taken City to be, where their Enemies are so unmerciful: I streight leapt off my Quilt, and ran into my Father's Room, for when by the cry I knew our Enemies to be entered, I expected to lose my Life, and therefore chose to lay it down by him who gave it me: I found him in a great Consternation, and hanging about his Neck, I expected the coming of our Enemies."

"The first who entered the Room was a *Spaniard;* for though I had never seen one before, I knew him to be one by his Dress, and a Helmet which he had on as soon as he entered, I left my Father, and fell at his Feet to beg both our Lives; and while I was in that posture, he bade his Souldiers stay back; but one of them cryed out, *'This is the Cupay',* (that is the Devil, or Conjurer) and advancing before the rest, ran at my Father with his Spear; the Commander immediately broke out of my Arms, which were clasped about his Knees, and, drawing a Pistol from under his Girdle, shot the *Indian* dead; and pulling out the other, he turned about to his Men, and swore that the first who disobeyed his Orders, as that Dog had done, he'd teach him what was the Discipline of a Souldier":

"While they stood all silent, amazed at the speedy Justice he had done on their Country-man, he came to me, who was lying on the Ground bemoaning my Father, whose Blood stained the Floor, he raised me from the Ground, and clapping a Guard of Souldiers on me, (with orders to keep us two from receiving any violence, upon pain of their Lives) he went away, I suppose, to help his Part'ners to take the other parts of the Town":

"Within an hour after he came back, and pulling a Box out of his Pocket, he took a Plaister out of it, and put it on my Father's wound, and bad me fear nothing; assuring me, that he did not come to destroy us, but to reduce us to a better Government; and as for me, he told me, that if I pleased, he would make me so happy, that I need not fear any danger, either of poverty, or Captivity, from the alteration of my condition: This, and the approach of day-light, did somewhat comfort me; my Father came to himself (for loss of blood had made him swoon) and began in the kindest words he could, to give thanks to the preserver of his Life, who was hugging and comforting me, when of a sudden we heard the same confused noise in the Streets, which we heard in the Night":

"I thought our Enemies were finishing their Cruelties upon

their Captives, and could not forbear bursting into Tears at their Miseries: The strange Commander endeavoured to comfort me all that he could, saying, That he could not help what the other Captains did to their Prisoners, but his own, and particularly my Father and I, should have no violence offered us":

"The noise grew louder and louder, as it drew nearer, when looking out of the Window, we perceived the *Antian* party driving the *Peruvians* before them, and before he could resolve what to do, they were killing his own Souldiers at the Door; he with a great deal of Courage leaped forward, and after all his men were kill'd defended the Door alone; and with his Spear laid the boldest of them dead at his feet: You will, perhaps, think that I was glad of this change of my Condition, to see my self unexpectedly freed, and my Countrymen revenged of their Enemies; but I'll assure you I was not; the danger which my generous Defender was in, weighed down all the Joy of the other, and though my fear made me for a while stand, as far as I could from the Weapons; yet, at last my desire to save him, overcame my Cowardise, and running to the door, I placed my self betwixt him and the Spears, which were bent against him; and cryed to my Father to speak to them to let him alone, my Father was so weak with the loss of Blood, that he could not come to the Door, but called to them with all the entreating words he could think on; most of them knew my Father and me, and having a great Veneration for us (as all our Nation has for their Priests) they gave over assaulting him":

"Only the foremost of them asked me, why I would defend one who was the Enemy both of our Country and Religion; I told them 'twas to him, that both their Priest and I owed our safety; that he kill'd the Man who hurt my Father, and with a great deal of care dressed his Wound; I desired therefore that, for our sakes, they would give me his Life: These words perswaded them to leave him to me; as soon as they were gone, I went out to see how things went, and brought him word, that a great Party from the Mountains, was come to our assistance, and that all who set foot on our Land were killed":

"'And, Madam' (said he) 'shall I be the only man who goes home, and carries the news of so great a defeat? Or shall it be said, that ever a Spaniard *let a Woman beg his Life of an Indian?*'"

"'Not of one Indian' (said I) 'for you were over-powered by numbers'":

"'No one but you' (said he) *should have given Astolfo his Life; but since I receive it from you, I'll make that use of it I should by serving you, and revenging my self of my Enemies, for this loss and disgrace I have suffered.*'"

"'I told him, that since he confessed his Life was mine, and that I had preserved it, it was not generous to use that Life against my Country; however, I left him to his liberty, and promised him, that at Night I would send him over in a Canoe to the other side":

"When Night came, I was as good as my word; and calling two trusty Men, I ordered them to row the Stranger over the River, telling them that his presence would be enough to secure them from the danger of their Enemies: At our parting he expressed himself very thankful to me for my generous usage of him, and told me, that e're long he would make me a return, in the mean he desired me to wear that about my Neck, pulling a Gold Medal, with a Chain of the same Metal: I, who had heard of the *Spanish* Covetousness, gave him a large Golden Wedge, and desiring him never to be my Country's Enemy, or put himself into the like danger."

"I took my leave, and left him to his Fortune; the Men came back before morning, and brought me word that they had set him safe on shore, and that all the other side of the River was covered with Men: This news, which they told about the Town, alarm'd us, and that Party which came down from the Mountains to our assistance, waited to receive them; some of our Scouts, who rowed as near the other side as they durst, brought us word that they had abundance of Canoes fill'd with Men, which made us think they design'd to Land by force, where the others had by Night; but this was but to amuse and draw our men that way; for they had provided a great number of Planks about 20 mile higher, and having lighted on a place where the River ran between two Hills, and therefore could not extend it self a quarter of a Mile, they made a floating Bridge, and on that they passed over some Men, before ours knew anything of it; they took such care to surprize the Natives, that no one came to bring us Intelligence of their being Landed, till some of the Planks which came floating down the River, made us suspect something; we sent some Scouts up the River, to discover what was the matter, and they brought word that the Enemy was on this side of the River:"

"Ours marched towards them as fast as they could to fight them, before any more came over, and having joyned Battel, the first news we heard, was of a great Victory, we had gained over them; and a great many Prisoners brought us, as the proof of its being true:"

"The *Indian* Prisoners were kept up to feed our Gods; but some few *Spaniards* that were taken, as being the Nobler Captives, were to be feasted on; as it was our Custom to tye our choice of Prisoners to a Tree, and a great Fire being made just by, the Priest was to cut off Slices from the more fleshy parts of them, and distribute them about to the People to broil and eat: If the Captive shewed any signs of pain, or groaned at his Sufferings, we counted him of a base Spirit; and after burning his Body, we scattered his Ashes in the Wind; but if he endured bravely to see his flesh eaten, we dryed the Sinews and Bones, and hanging them upon the Mountains, we deify'd them, and went Pilgrimages to them.

"There were ten *Spaniards* brought to my Father, and two or 300 *Indians*, who were all tyed, and secured by a Guard set over them; the *Indians* to be a Prey to the Bellies of our Gods, and the *Spaniards*, to those of our Souldiers: As soon as they were brought in, my Curiosity prompted me to see them, but very little to my satisfaction; for the first I set my Eyes on was he whom I had set at liberty before: I was both concerned and amazed to see him there, and uncertain whether I should do any thing in his favour or no; therefore I pretended not to know him; till he making as low a bow as his being tyed would permit, asked me, did I not know him whose Life I had saved?"

"'Are you he', *said I*, 'whom I set free but a few days ago? I thought your good usage might have made you our Friend, or at least your dangerous escape might have been a fair warning to you; but since you are the second time come amongst our Enemies, and are still plotting my destruction, you shall suffer for your ingratitude, and to shew how little I pity you, I will go to see you Sacrificed, and eat the first bit of you my self.'"

"'As for the danger of coming again' *(answered he)* 'a *Spaniard* fears none, but I was so far from plotting your destruction, that I hung that Medal about your Neck for my Souldiers to know you by; I had indeed a design upon your Countrey; but for you, my greatest desire was, by saving you and your Family, to shew how much I aimed to ingratiate my self into your favour.'"

"'These are all but Wheedles' *(said I)* 'to save your Life; but they shall not serve'":

"'No, they shall not' *(said he)* 'for since you can entertain such mean thoughts as these of me, I scorn to take my Life; all the repentance my attempt has brought upon me is, that is has displeased you; I thought to have requited you for giving me liberty, and to have made you amends for the loss of your Country, by bringing you to a better, but since this ill success has prevented me, all that I desire, is to dye in your favour':

"'The way to do that' *(reply'd I)* 'is to dye undaunted, for then you shall be one of our Gods'":

"'I will do so' *(said he)* 'be you there, and shew but the least sign of pity at my death, and I'll go off with such a Courage, that him whom you slighted whilst he was alive, you shall adore when he is dead.'"

"Though in a Man's mouth who was at liberty, this would have looked like a Boast, yet coming from one who did not know but he might suffer next day, it appear'd so brave, that I could not but admire it: The others held their Tongues, but looked so fierce, as if they kept silence out of disdain":

"I went thence with a great opinion of their Courage, and a secret horrour in my self at the cruelty of our Nation, which gave brave Men such barbarous usage: I called to mind his professing a design to save me, and carry me to a happier place; and his telling me of the thing about my Neck, for a Token to know me by, made me believe it was true; and when I considered of this, I imagined I ought to save his Life, but I could not tell how to do it without my Father's consent:"

As I came into the Room where he lay ill of his Wound, there was one brought him word of the death of his only Son; who was found after the Battel among the Slain, with a Bullet lying in him: I shewed my sorrow in all the extravagancies which our Nation commits on the like occasions; but my Father only gave a groan or two, as it were to rouze up his anger, and said, that he would comfort himself for his Son, in revenging his Death, since all his grief could never raise him to Life again: That all the *Spaniards* who were in the Battel were killed, except ten who were in his Custody, and he would sacrifice each of them, because he would be sure that his Sons Murderer should not escape; for since he was killed with a Bullet, he did not doubt but it was a Spaniard shot him.

"We lay all that Night awake grieving for my Brother, but the next day, when the first Fury of our grief was over, and my Father began to talk with me about our Prisoners:"

"'Suppose, Father,' *(said I)* 'the *Spaniard* who saved our Lives should be one of them?'"

"'If that should come to pass,' *(said my Father)* 'he had better staid where he was, than come over to seek his Death here the second time':"

"'But, Sir,' *(said I)* 'gratitude would oblige us to save his Life, who saved ours first:'"

"'That we have done already' *(said my Father)* 'and so we have returned his kindness; and if after so hard an escape he should be come again, he does not deserve his Life, neither would I be guilty of so much injustice to my Son and my Countrey, as to save that Man's Life, who has been the Death of the one, and has made a second attempt to be the Destruction of the other.'"

"This arguing of my Fathers seemed so reasonable, and his Indignation so just, that I could not gain-say it, and therefore said no more to him, but went back to my Prisoner, and told him, that I did intend to save him, and his Companions for his sake; but that my Brother's Body being found shot, had so incensed my Father, that I could not prevail with him to spare them; and therefore I told them they must prepare their Courage to dye, as soon as my Father's Wounds would suffer him to assist at the Solemnity."

"'Well,' *(says he)* 'since I must dye, and it does not lye in your power to help it, I am sorry you told me you attempted it, for that shews so much kindness, that it makes me desirous to live: I was willing to dye when you upbraided me with the begging my life, but now I can no longer be suspected to flatter you out of any such hopes, since you say it is not in your power to help me; I own that my Death is no grievance to me, only as it prevents my living for you; and all that I'll now desire of you, is to let me dye the first, that I may not behold the Cruelties exercised on my Countrymen.'"

"The Love and Courage which I perceived in these words, quite altered the thoughts I had, of giving him up to my Father's resentments; and from that time I found something within me so strong on his side, that it over-ballanced the Duty I should have paid to my Father's will, and my Brother's Blood: I went to my Father, and told him that he who saved his Life was there, and urged to him how ingrateful we should be, if we did not restore him to his Liberty; but my Father answered me with the same Arguments he had done before":

"Then I endeavoured to corrupt him that was Captain of the Guard that looked to them, but he was a Blood-thirsty violent natured Man, and not only refused me, but complained to my Father, who was so angry, that I should endeavour to release so many of our worst, our most formidable Enemies, the Spaniards, that he threaten'd, the next time I attempted the like, he would have me condemned to suffer with them, as the Enemy of my Country. I knew his violent temper too well to venture any farther, and gave over all hopes of saving my Prisoner":

"The next morning four *Indians* were to be carried to our Gods to feed upon, they drew Lots for their Lives, they were blind-folded when they drew, and I held the Cistern, and decided who the Lot fell upon, and it often grieved me to doom the poor trembling Slaves; my Prisoner seeing me picking out some of them for Death, told me, he longed to know when his turn would come; I told him that his must come as well as the rest; that I had incurred my Father's displeasure on his account, and left nothing undone which I thought might be for his safety, that I hoped this was all he could expect, and desired him to own before his Death that I was out of his debt; yet I had resolved with my self to keep him till the last, in hopes that before that time the Guards might be changed, or else my Father's anger might be mitigated, when most of them had been sacrificed to it:"

"Two or three days had now past over, in which time my Father had given the Guards particular charge to beware of the *Spaniards*, for fear I should free them; the day came that he found himself well enough to perform the Sacrifice, and our *Spaniards* were brought out in the midst of their Guards, to draw Lots which of them should make our Banquet; by ill chance it fell on my Prisoner; I changed the Lot, and sentenced one of the others in his stead, but not so cleverly but that my Father perceived it: The poor wretch was cut to pieces slice after slice, and lived long enough to see his own Flesh broiled, and eaten by the Company; you must think this was a terrible sight to the rest, who saw by their Companion what they were to suffer."

"I expected to keep him the same way I had the first day, and went on the morrow with the same design, little dreaming what would happen; for my Father, who had seen me play the Jugler the day before, would hold the Pitcher himself, and the first black Lot was again drawn by my Prisoner: Upon that the Fire was made to broil his Flesh, he was stript naked, and tyed to the Tree; he looked about him, without as much as changing Countenance at his Destiny; but when he turned his Eyes towards me he blushed, I believe out of shame, to think that I should see him in that helpless condition: Such a sight as this, which would have drawn pity even from a merciful Enemy; what effect then do you think it had upon one that loved him? Or rather, what effect had it not? I blusht and grew pale, Anger, Love, and Fear, succeeded one another; Anger at the Barbarity of my Countreymen, Love for him, and Fear at his danger: But just as my

The Irish *Princess*

Father's Knife fetched Blood from the brawny part of his Arm (the place which he first began with) I was not able to bear up any longer, but fell in a swoon; which my Father perceiving, left him, and catched me in his Arms; but not having yet recovered strength enough to bear me up, he fell to the Ground with me, and lighting upon his Wound, rubbed the Plaisters off, and made it bleed afresh:"

"My Father was immediately taken up on some of their Shoulders, and carried home, and every one said 'twas an unlucky day, and the Gods were angry, so the Sacrifice was deferred till the next."

'When I came to my self, I was very glad to see the poor Man delivered from immediate death, though it cost some of my Father's blood, but it almost distracted me, to think what a short reprieve I had for him, only till the next day; his Fate was now at its Crisis, and within twenty four hours I must either see him free, or mangled to pieces; all my former hopes lay in deferring the time till another Guard came, which perhaps I could have bribed off, or till my Father's mind was altered; but his Anger continued still; and because he found the Captain of the Guard as violent against the *Spaniards* as himself, he ordered him to continue in the same Post, till all the *Spaniards* were Sacrificed: My poor Prisoner's Lot was come, and he to dye the next day, and I had not yet thought on any way that could prevent it:"

"After having wracked my Invention a great while, for a way to free him, at last I lighted on this: There were two of my Father's Servants, whom I sent formerly to row my Prisoner over the River; I knew they wished well to him, because when he enter'd our House as an Enemy, he had saved their Lives; these two I acquainted with my design to release him: I gave them a large Pot full of pleasant Liquor, made of our Sacred Plant the *Coca*, and bade them towards Night to bring that to the Guard-house, as a present from my Father:"

"Our Guard consisted of a hundred Men, for the preservation of the Temple, and the treasures of it, and the Prisoners who belonged to it; so that all these things might well require the care of an hundred Men: We had near twice the number of *Indian*

Prisoners, besides the nine *Spaniards*, only they were Armed, these were naked and tied:"

"Out of the Temple I had got Arms enough for them all, and conveyed them into a Room hard by, to be ready upon occasion; when the two Servants came with the Liquor, all the Souldiers crowded into the Guard-house, only two who stood to their Arms at the Prison Door; when the Servants saw them all engaged about the drink, they left the Guard, and came to give me notice; upon which I took some Daggers (which our Souldiers had taken from the *Spaniards*, and hung up in the Temple as Trophies) these I hid under my Gown, (for the Women of our Nation had thin silk Gowns to wear in the cool of the Night) and so under pretence of seeing the Prisoners, I conveyed these unto them: When I came in I saw my Prisoner asleep, I cut the Cords of his Hands and Legs, and as I cut them he awaked and found himself loose; thence I went to another, and still as I loosened them I put a Dagger in their Hands: I told them I was come to give them all Liberty, if they would shew themselves men, and Conquer an Enemy whom they would find surprized, and not ready to oppose them."

"'And my Astolfo' (said I) 'I have done all this for your sake, yet I will rather stay behind you, and undergo all the punishments that an angry Father, or incensed Town could inflict upon me, than fly with you, unless you are as willing to receive me, as I to go.' Several of the *Indians* wept for Joy, and the *Spaniards*, for all their Gravity, could scarce forbear it:"

"My Prisoner said, that he was more glad of my Love, than of the saving his Life, and would have told me abundance of the like nature, had he not been interrupted; for one of the Centinels, not liking my long stay, came to see what was the matter, and no sooner came in but was stabb'd by one of the *Spaniards*; my two Servants had stood all this while at the Door, and when one of the Centinels left them to come to us, they dispatched the other; by this time the *Indians* had untyed one another, and I carried them to a Chamber hard by, where I had laid the Arms:"

"Some of the Guard, hearing a noise, chanced to come out, and mistrusting something more than ordinary alarm'd the rest, but they came a little of the latest, for we had as many Armed as they; they began a very bloody Engagement, and a great many were killed on both sides, but our number increasing we over-powered them, and they fled every way for safety."

"My Prisoner had given me in charge to some of the *Indians*, who were formerly under his Command, and they kept me in Rear till the Guard fled: Then *Astolfo* came to me, and desired me to come down to the River side, before the Town Guards came upon us, for our noise had alarm'd the Town; and there were at that time five or six thousand Men which were left with us, for fear those on the other side the River should make another Invasion; but we were too quick for the uproar, before the Guards came we got to the River, and there being abundance of Canoes, and the Enemy coming after us, you may guess we did not stand to Complement who should take Boat first:

"The eight *Spaniards*, *Astolfo*, the two *Indians* and my self, took the same Canoe: We put off altogether as fast as we could, but in a little time we were parted from the rest, the night being so dark that we knew not which way we went, though the Wind blew so hard from the other side, that we were afraid 'twould force us on our Enemies Coast, to our ruin:

"Two of our *Spaniards* tugg'd against it as hard as they could, till one of them broke his Oar, and then we gave over striving, and let the Boat go down which way the River would carry it; the next morning we would have made for Shore, but having but one Oar the Wind beat us off, and carried us down all that day and the next night with the Stream. Though the first day we got away we were very chearful, yet now wanting Provisions, and being driven down we knew not whither, dampt the Joy we should otherwise have taken in our Love and Liberty:

"I began to reflect on my former actions, and to think this a just punishment for my undutiful leaving my Father, and my Country; I began to grow faint with hunger, and he was so troubled to see me in that condition, that in the greatest danger of his Life I never saw him shew so much sorrow. The farther we Sailed the River still grew wider and wider; on one side we could not Land, because the Wind would not let us, on the other side we durst not, because 'twas inhabited by those Nations who are mortal Enemies to the *Spaniards:*"

"We were now come down a great way, and the River had turned so, that the Wind, which before was against us, now was for us; we made towards the Land with the greatest haste that a violent Hunger could make; as we came near the Shore we discovered a Boat lying under a Rock, we made towards it, and saw only one Man in it, and he was asleep, so that we were upon him before he awaked; he would have resisted, but finding it in vain for one Man to fight with eleven, he yielded up himself and his Boat; in it we found store of Victuals (the richest prize we could have wished for at that time) and you may think we fell on to some purpose:"

"We examined the Fellow, and he said he belonged to a Ship which lay about sixty Leagues lower; that they sent twenty Men up the River in quest of a Prize which they were to take, by plundering a little Town thereabouts; he told us, that there were about so many more left in the Ship, but that the greatest part of them lay sick of the Wounds they had received in a late Engagement:"

"We stept into his Boat, and going down the River, in eight days time we came within sight of the Ship; then having got out of the Man what intelligence we thought necessary, we threw him over-board, and made up to the side of the Pinnace; it being duskish, and they knowing their own Boat again, they mistook us for their own Men; so that half the *Spaniards* entered, and had killed all that were above Deck, before they mistrusted any thing; the rest they took Prisoners, and (throwing all the Wounded Men into the Sea) because we had not Provisions sufficient to last us all, they set their Prisoners on Shore, and so came down the River merrily in a Ship of our own:"

"The *Spaniards* fell to searching, and found some Bullion in her, besides a vast deal of ready money, which, after a just division between us ten, we computed would amount to near 30000 Ducats a piece, so that with a general consent we Sail'd streight for *Spain*, intending to Land at the first Port of that Kingdom which we came to."

The Irish *Princess*

"Now we were happy enough, we had escaped our Enemies the *Indians*, and Famine, which had like to have proved a more fatal Enemy than they; besides the Prize which enriched us beyond our expectation, and came in good time to help my needy Fortune, who in that hurry of leaving home, had not remembered to bring any thing of value with me, besides a few Pearl which I always wore about me."

"My Servant came and took me in his Arms, congratulating my escape out of the several dangers we had been in, and thanking me a thousand times for the kindness I had shewed in saving his Life; and more for leaving a Father, to run the same Fortune with him: In fine, he promised that he would requite all my kindnesses, by having me Christened, and marrying me as soon as we came to *Spain*:"

"And I was so well pleased with the alteration of my Condition so much for the better, that I think that Night was one of the pleasantest of my Life."

"The next Morning we spy'd a Sail making up to us, and as soon as it came within reach, it sent a great Shot to command us to strike Sail; we saw by the bulk that it was a Man of War, too strong for us to resist:"

"We, much against our wills, staid for it, and received some of them on board; in searching our Ship they found divers Colours, as Pyrats usually have; our Vessel, it seems, had been one, and for their Faults who had owned her, we were all seiz'd, our Vessel made a Prize, and our men taken Prisoners: The Man of War being a *Spaniard*, the Captain said he would reserve *Astolfo* and his eight Country-men to be tryed on Shore, and condemned to the Gallies: My two *Indians* (notwithstanding all my intreaties for their Lives) he hanged on the Ropes before my Face: But taking compassion on me, he said he would keep me to wait on his Wife:"

"Accordingly, when we came upon the Coasts of *Spain*, he sent the nine *Spaniards* Prisoners to *Sevil*; and though I begg'd him to let me accompany *Astolfo*, he kept me at Sea a few days more, and then Landed me at *Aveiro*, and gave me a present to a Wife he had there."

"It would be tedious for me to tell you how ill I bore this worst change of my Fortune; I raged, I grieved, till my Sighs and Tears grew so thick upon one another, that no one could know which was the most plentiful of their two Fountains, my Heart, or my Eyes."

"My Mistress, who was a good natur'd Gentlewoman, interessed her self in my Sorrows, and would often enquire what was the reason of my grieving; till at last her Importunities drew from me the whole Relation, which I have now made to you; she bade me be comforted, and think no more of him; I told her I could not be satisfied without him:"

"'That opinion' (says she) 'is, I hope, a false one; you must be comforted either without him, or not at all, for you must never expect to see him again; for supposing he should escape, being condemned to the Gallies, yet how is it likely that you, who are a Stranger, should find out a single Man, and one of no note, in such a large City as Sevill, or one who perhaps, before you could get thither, would be gone to some other part of the World?'"

"I told her I had an Art, by which I could do more than that; and thus much I knew, that if I were at my liberty, and had a little travelling Money, I should not be a year e're I found him. She asked what Art that was":

"''Tis what I learned from my Father' (said I) 'and is very common among us'":

"She desired to see the effects of it; I told her I would shew it, in resolving whatever question she would ask me. She bade me tell her where her Husband was at that time, and when he would come home: I told her she must buy me a small Drum, which had never been used before, and I would then tell her that question, and any other. When she heard me affirm it so confidently, she said she would try me, and bought me a Drum:"

"I that Night used some Charms over it, which my Father and I had practised on such occasions; and the next morning I told her my Master would be at home on the morrow":

"'I thought (says she)' (laughing) 'how you could foretell: Why your Master is gone into the Straights cruising, and bade me not expect him these two Months.'"

"I let her enjoy her incredulity, but she had like to have suffered by it; for she, good Woman, considering that her Captain made long stays and short returns, had providently looked out for a Gallant, to comfort her in his absence; but I was yet too much a Stranger to me made acquainted with such privacies. She had an old *Spanish* Maid, who was the only Servant she kept, till I came; this Maid was privy to all her Intrigues."

"They had at that time pitched upon a young Gentleman, who had an Estate near the City, he was very fond of my Mistress, as men usually are of every new Conquest, and had invited her to spend a few days, in her Husband's absence, at his Countrey Seat: She consented to go with him, and they had assigned a day to go together, and as it happened, 'twas the very day after that on which my Master was to come home; but it drawing towards Night, and my Mistress hearing no news of him, nor seeing any likelihood of his coming, she sent her Maid to invite the Gallant to Sup with her; me she sent up to Bed, pretending that she had some business for me to rise very early the next morning:"

"I lay in the Room over her, and though I went to Bed without the suspition of any such treachery against my Master, yet chance discovered it all to me":

"I awakened after I thought I had been a pretty while asleep, I fancied I heard a Man's voice in my Mistresses Chamber, and concluded it was my Master's, because I thought my Art would not deceive me; however, my curiosity prompted me to a desire of knowing whether it was he or no":

"I got out of Bed softly, and looking down, I saw her sitting at Table, with three dishes of Meat before her; (in which hungry *Spain* is a noble Treat) by her there was seated a fine young Gentleman, he whom I just now described to you; their discourse, at that instant, happened to be of me. She told him she had a Slave who pretended to foretell future events; that she had told her that the Captain would be at home that day; the Gentleman laughed, as he said, to think that a Slave should be so bold, to impose such a Story on her Mistress; he laughed at her too, for giving any belief to me; and I laughed at them both, to think how secure they fancied they were from my Eyes and my Masters, and yet how much they were mistaken."

"While I was peeping down, and listening to their discourse, we heard a loud knocking at the Door; my Mistress cry'd out immediately that it was the Captain's knock, and that she was undone, unless they could hide him somewhere in that Room; for to send him up to mine, was the way to let me know of it, and being a Stranger, perhaps I might betray him to her Husband."

"The Gentleman was young and slender; and his Limbs, which seemed composed rather for Love than War, shew'd that he was a very unequal Match for a great two-handed Sea Captain: And you have all heard enough of the raging Spanish Jealousie, to think, that if a young handsome Man had been found there, and at so suspitious a time, 'twould have gone near to have cost all three of them their Lives."

"The Captain still knocking harder and harder, made them all at their wits end what to do with him; at length they bethought themselves of a great Chest, which my Master had given his Wife full of Plunder, when he first came on shore with me; but she had taken all those things out, and my Master had filled it with Sea Bisket, which he had bought for his Men; the Mistress and Maid emptyed these Biskets out under the Bed, and begg'd the Gentleman to try whether he could get into the Chest; the young Spark was as complying as she could with him; he made a quick shift to get in, and his Fear was at that time so strong upon him, that it would not only have driven him into that, but into a Mouse-hole, if there had been one in the Room:"

"As soon as he was in, the Maid let in my Master, who seemed a little angry that he was kept so long at the door; and seeing the Cloath laid, and the Table covered with Meat, he asked my Mistress how all that came there, and what she designed with it? I wondered how she would come off; but she very readily answered, that she provided it for him, and kept him at the Door while she took it from the Fire, that he might be the more surprized, to find so good a Supper ready for him on the Table."

"He asked how she could provide it for him, since no Man in

Aveiro knew of his coming? My Mistress answered, that the *Indian* he had left with her, had told her he would certainly be at home that night."
"When did she tell you this?" (said he)
"Yesterday'"(answered my Mistress).
"Then, by St. *Jago, She is a Witch,*" (said my Master) *"for yesterday morning, till the Storm came, I did not know* (that I should come) *my self':*"
"I hope, Captain," said my Mistress, "you have received no damage by the Storm'":
"None,"said he, "but the spoiling my store of Bisket, which got wet, and my poor Men are in want of it; but I will have you" said he (turning to a Cabbin-Boy that waited on him, *'go now and call two or three of our Men on Shore, that we may have hands enough to carry that Chest of Bisket to the Water-side:*
"Time enough for that to morrow, Love," (said my Mistress)
"'No,' (says my Master) *'my Men are in present want of it, and I ought to take care of them, as well as of my self.'*"
"The Boy went on his Errand, and my Mistress with a great deal of pain, waited the unlucky coming of the Seamen to carry the Chest away, and her Jewel that was in it."
"I had till this time been an unconcern'd Spectator, and only pleased my self with the sight my Master's coming had put them in, but now I saw I must help them out, or they had no way of their own to bring them off; dressing my self therefore as fast as I could, I went down to them; my Mistress, I believe, wondred to see me there, and she thought I was asleep, yet she did take no publick notice of it, lest my being sent up to Bed, should give my Master the greater cause to suspect something."
"After bidding my Master wellcome home, I turned to my Mistress: 'And did I not tell you, Madam,' *(said I)* 'that my Master would be at home to Night?'"
"'You may see,' *(said she)* 'by my preparations for him, that I believed you':"
"I could not forbear smiling to see how she would have imposed on me, as she did on my Master: 'But, Madam,' *(answered I)* 'since I have given you such a proof of my skill,

which (though it has told you this only for tryals sake yet) hereafter may shew it self some way, which may prove more serviceable to you, I would desire one favour of you in its behalf':

"'What's that?' (*answered she*)"

"'Tis' (*said I*) 'that you would pardon me for an accident which befell me in the performance of it':"

"'What's that' (*says she*) 'I hope you have not raised any Spirits that have broken our Windows, or done any damage to the House':"

"'What if they have' (*said my Master*) 'you shall pardon any slight mischief that they have done':"

"'They have done no mischief at all,' (*said I*) 'pray do not be affrighted, Madam, and I'll tell you all: When you were abroad yesterday I set about my Enchantment, to answer your question, but you came home a little too soon, while I was asking some questions concerning my own Fortune; hearing you at the Door, and not having time to lay that Spirit which I had raised, I ordered him to throw the Bisket out of the Chest, and enter into it himself; you can't but have heard how mischievous Spirits are while they are at liberty, and to preventy any such mischief, I confined him there, till your absence should give me leisure to lay him: You went soon after to Bed, and I durst not tell you how near the Spirit was to you, for fear of fright'ning you, nor would at all, had not the present use my Master has of the Chest, forced me to this discovery':"

"When my Mistress heard this told, she ran to my Master, and clasping him about the middle, pretended to be in the greatest fright imaginable; and desired him to leave me the House to my self, till I had ridded the house of the Devil. Though the hot Supper, which my Master believed prepared for him, and my Mistress saying, that 'twas because I foretold his coming, had confirmed him in the belief of my Art; and the earnestness with which I begg'd pardon, made him not question what I said to be true; yet he laughed at the extream fear, which his Wife so excellently counterfeited, and said, 'Never fear, Wife, that Mr. Devil, who has been so civil as to lye there all last night, will be so rude, as to disturb us now: Sure, *Faniaca*, he will not force us to leave our Victuals to cool, to dance attendance on him: If he will give us leave to Sup, we will retire afterwards, and give you leisure to dismiss him':"

"'Not for the World,' (*said my Mistress*) 'I cannot eat one bit, nor enjoy my self one minute, while the Devil is so near us; dear Love, consider the danger 'tis to be here, and let us go to some Neighbours, and leave the Witch and the Devil together':"

"'Since you are so fearful' (*said my Master*) 'have but patience, till my Men come, and I'll order them to carry the Chest up Stairs, for I am loath to leave this hot Supper; but do not shew your fear to them, for if they know that his Devilship is in it, 'tis likely they won't venture to meddle with it.'"

"My Mistress said, she thought it long till they came; and I dare swear she did not counterfeit in that, but was at that time as desirous to get rid of her inclosed Spark, as ever she was to get into his Company: The Sea-men kept her not long in pain, for they came while we were talking of them: My Master mentioned nothing of the Bisket to them, but desired, before he sat down, that they would remove that Chest up one pair of Stairs for him:"

"Two of them immediately laid hold on two Rings which were fastened in the sides of it, and heaved it be degrees up stairs, I lighting them the way; the Stairs were so narrow that they could not go both on a breast, but one pulled the Chest up, and the other heav'd it after him, by which means our Gallant was almost stifled in it, for his Head chanced to lie at that end which was lowermost; therefore, when it was near the top, he not being able to endure it any longer, stirred about to lye easier, and coughed; at which the Men, being startled, let go, and the weight of the Chest tumbled it down that pair of Stairs, and another pair which joined just to it; though the Chest was locked, yet the tumbling of it made me expect every moment that it would fly open; and therefore, lest it should discover the Gentleman, I dropt the Candle: My Mistress shriek'd at the noise, and clapt too the Room Door where my Master was; he stood silent, not knowing what to think of the noise; one of the

Sea-men stood by me till the Maid brought us a light, but the other, who bore up the lower end of the Chest, was driven down all the Stairs before it:"

"I heard the poor Man groan, and was terribly afraid that it was the Gentleman's voice, and that the fall had crippled him; I therefore desired them all to stay in the Room while I went down Stairs, they were willing to obey me, for the horrid noise had put them in such a Fright, that they stood gazing one at another, wondering what the event would be: When I came down, I found the Chest open, and the Gentleman gone; then I helped the hurt Man up Stairs; his head was broken, and some parts of his Body bruised with the fall, but he was more afraid than hurt."

"'Well,' said my Mistress to me, 'this comes of your raising the Devil.'"

"The Seaman, who did not know what to make of it before, hearing her say it was the Devil, concluded it was so indeed; and said, He was sure 'twas a cloven Foot trod on him, for he felt it, and that he saw the Tail of it, as it went out of the House."

"'What, then is he gone' (said my Mistress)."

"'Yes, Madam, he is gone' (said I) 'and shall trouble you no more':"

"'A good riddance' (said she) 'of your Mischievous Spirits, pray raise no more of them':"

"'Then, Madam,' (said I) 'you must not give me the occasion.'"

"Now my Mistress's real fear was over, her counterfeit one vanished with it, and bidding us set Chairs, she and my Master sat down; the wounded Man he sent on Ship-board to the Chyrurgeon, and having supped and diverted himself with the poor imprisoned Devil, they went to Bed, where he passed that night with my Mistress, who would rather have had that Devil for her Bedfellow."

"The next morning my Mistress's Confessor came to her; and my Master, who was filled with the last nights adventure, could not contain himself from communicating it to the Father, saying, That he had given his Wife an *Indian*, that could raise Spirits, and make them tell her things that were doing at ever so great a distance; relating, withall, what had happened by that means in his House the night before: The Holy Man, stroking up his Beard, with an austere look, told him, that this was no Jest, said, it was making a compact with the Devil, and that his Christianity obliged him to confess himself an Enemy to all such actions; and therefore was bound in Conscience to discover this to the Fathers of the Inquisition; and desired my Master to secure me:"

"He said this when I was by; I was earnest to know what he meant by the Inquisition; but when he told me the danger of coming under the clutches of that bloody Court, and named some of their Punishments, as the Wheel, Immuring, and other ingenious Cruelties of theirs, I would have given my life for a *Maravedy*."

"When my Master was gone out, I fell down on my knees to my Mistress, and begg'd her to give me my liberty, and put me in some way to escape this barbarous tryal, that the Priest would bring me to: I told her I was loath to mention the kindness I had done her, in conveying her Spark away, lest that should look like upbraiding her with it; but thus much I must say of it, that it was that Story which made the Priest so zealous against me, and that if ever I came before the Inquisition, Self-preservation would force the truth from me, and that I must confess the Cheat I put upon my Master, to avoid the imputation of Witchcraft."

"She answered me very civilly, that she had such a sense of the kindness I had done her, that she would requite it with giving me my freedom; and when my Master came home, she was very urgent till she prevailed with him to do the like; whether she did this out of gratitude to me, or the fear of my threatning a discovery, I do not know; but my Master called me to him, and bade me go and hide my self on board that night, lest the Officers should come to search for me:"

"The next day he came on board himself, and asked me where I would rather Land, I told him in *England*; for I had consulted my Drum, and was informed, that I should find my lover in one of the Northern Islands, coming from the Siege of a City, and the Rumour of the *Hollanders* just then Landing in *England*, made me think that likely to be the place:"

"We met at Sea with an *English* Merchant, and giving me a little Money, he put me on board there; I had, besides, some Money my Mistress gave me at parting, and a Pearl Necklace, with some Bracelets, which my Master (finding so great a Prize with us) spared me, when he plundered me at Sea; these sold in *England* for two hundred Duckets; with some of this Money I put my self into an *English* Garb, keeping my *Spanish* one by me, and went up to *London*, and hired my self to a Person of Quality; and being an Outlandish Woman, and appearing in a very gentile Dress, I was made her Gentlewoman; I staid with her near a year, in which time I put up a little more Money, and good Cloaths, and learn'd *English* enough, and then I left her, to travel in quest of my Lover:"

"I went down to *Chester*, and hearing that there was a War in *Ireland*, I embarked for this Kingdom; I have been in *Dublin*, and am now come hither to follow the Camp, where I am assured I shall find him:"

"I get as much as maintains me on the Road, by telling Fortunes to the Gentry, who sometimes are very liberal to me: Amongst the different Fates I read, those belonging to Love delight me most, as being most agreeable to my own temper; and when ever it lies in my way to forward any of those by my Skill, my being in their Circumstances, makes me the readier to help them."

"She ended thus, to the admiration of all the Company, whose Ears were tyed to the Story: The Prince, who was pleas'd with the Wit of the *Indian*, could not deny her those praises that were due to it; and from her ingenuity in the management of her intrigue, and her constancy in continuing if so long, he concluded that the *Spaniard* must needs be happy in her; and told her, that if he was in the Army, whether he were in Commission, or a private Souldier, he would do what lay in his power to contribute to the finding him out for her:"

"But, he said, he expected a kindness of her in retaliation, and that if he searched for her Lover, she would (if need were) do him the same service; that he never gave any credit to Gypsies, or any other Vagabonds that pretended to her Talent, but since she had proved her Skill in so exemplary a manner, he would lay aside his former incredulity, and desire she would satisfy his Curiosity in some things, which it would conduce to his quiet to know. The *Indian* said, she would wait on his Highness, at his Lodgings, the next day, and give him what satisfaction her Art could afford him."

"But he was not the only Person that wanted her assistance, neither had the terrours of War so frighten'd Love, as to make him wholly abdicate his power over that Kingdom; but in this Ball he had some Votaries of both Sexes, and the ingenious *Indian* told publickly the place where she Lodged, that those whose Modesty restrained them from speaking to her there, might have a more private opportunity."

"The Prince went home well satisfied with the hopes of knowing his Fortune, and told *Celadon* that he was so impatient to see the next day, and the *Indian* that would satisfie his Doubts, that he found himself not the least inclinable to Sleep; therefore, if he would make him a Song, in answer to that, which he told him he had over-heard his Mistress singing at the Well, he would that Night go Serenade her with it; and though he could neither meet with her at the Ball, nor find her at home, yet this Song would make a discovery which might alter the reservedness of her Behaviour: *Celadon* made one; about Midnight they sallied out together, and stopping under her Window, the Prince, with the best air which his Guittar and Voice could frame, began this Song, to the same Tune which she had Sung to hers.

> THe Souldier yields his vanquish'd Heart,"
> As Conqu'ring Beauty's prize;
> And though he fears no mortal Dart,
>   The Thunder of your Frowns he flyes,
>   And dreads the Lightning of your Eyes.

"*You shall dread this more,*" said a Voice interrupting him; the

Prince looking about, to see whence the Voice came, saw three naked Swords making towards him: *Celadon* came up immediately to his assistance; it being so dark, that neither Party could see to defend themselves, there had been fair work in a small time, if some of the Guards walking the round, had not been pretty near them; when they came up, the three fled, and the Souldiers knowing the Prince, Congratulated his Highness's escape, from a Death, which the most unskillful Enemy might have given him, when there was not light enough to allow him fair play for his Life: They would needs wait on him home, and he considering that the noise might have allarm'd some of the Neighbours, thought it best to retire, for fear of raising a discourse, which might prove prejudicial to his Mistress, and offend her."

"The next Afternoon the two Strangers came to wait on the Prince, and finding him alone, one of them told him, she was come to make good her promise, that she brought her Companion with her, who understood nothing but *Spanish;* however, if his Highness had any secret extraordinary to communicate to her, she would go with him to another end of the Room; the Prince opening a Closet Door, retired in thither with her, and opened his mind in these words:"

"Since I want such advice, as cannot rightly be given, without some fore-knowledge of what will be the issue of it, and since my business is nothing but an Amour, who so fit to consult about it as you, who are a Fortune-teller, and a Lover too? You may understand then, that my business is nothing but Love; it is one so violent, and yet so unreasonable, that I am unable to curb it, nor have I any hopes of success, if I let it go on; and 'tis just with me now, as with a Souldier, whom his too boyling Valour has engaged so far in the Battel, that his Enemies have surrounded him; there's no retreating for him, because the Foe is behind, nor any likelihood of breaking through, because there are too many before him:"

"So am I surrounded with difficulties, pushed forward by Love, and opposed by Despair; carried on by her Charms, and driven back by her Disdain; now I would know what my success may be, if I go on, and accordingly I will either nourish this Passion, or tear it from my Breast?"

"I cannot see", (*said the* Indian) "what should discourage your Highness from proceeding, since there are those perfections in your Highness, which give you desert enough to pretend to the best of Woman: I fancy your Highness has fallen in Love with some one below you, and that your Love and Ambition are at variance, whether that shall draw Love up, or Love draw that down: I know these two generally tend two contrary ways, the one, like Earth, descending, the other, like Fire, still aspiring upwards."

"You guess as right, (*said the Prince*) as if you had seen my Heart; and if you can tell me how I shall succeed in my Love, I'll make that, or my Ambition, conform it self to the other: I doat on one who is beneath me; when I made my first Addresses, she seemed Pliant enough, as if she had no aversion to my Love; nay, I over-heard her once confessing to a Confident, that she had a kindness for me; and when I thought her my own, I found my self most deceived; for some Capricio or other made her, that she would never since admit me into her Company; I went several times to enquire for her at home, but the Servant still shifted me off, either denying her, or pretending she was sick; I contrived last Night's Ball, in hopes to entice her thither, but it failed; I Serenaded her last Night with a Song, in answer to one I heard her Sing, that time she confessed a Love for me, but before it was ended, I was interrupted by some Night Adventurer, who attempted to kill me, which makes me suspect 'tis some Rival; inform me by your Art, whether this is a Favourite that supplants me in her Heart, or whether it be Virgin Niceness, Hypocritical Modesty, or what else it is that has put this sudden stop to my Success?"

"This is a puzzling question (*said the* Indian) but give me one Night's time to consult my Drum about it, and I will bring you an answer."

"The Prince seemed well contented, and the two Strangers, taking their leaves of him, left him to expect the insight the next day would give him of his Fortune."

On the morrow they came again, and the Prince took the *Indian* into the Closet (as he had done the day before) and desired her to be as plain as she could, in foretelling him all that was to befall him in his Love:

"*First,*" *(said she)* "your Highness must acquaint me whether you design Marriage, or no."

"Marriage!" *(said the Prince)* "why did not I confess to you, that she was a private Gentlewoman, one beneath me? I wonder you should ask such a question:"

"Pray, Sir, be not angry," *(reply'd the* Indian) "for how can I tell your Highness what success you are like to have in any design, until I know the design it self?"

"If" *(answer'd he)* I can enjoy her on any terms, but those of Marriage, I shall think my self very happy; if not, my Love has so wholly blinded me, as to make me forget my Interest, and my Honour."

"Your Highness *(said she)* is certainly very prudent, in having so great a command over your Love; and pray make use of it, when I shall tell you the state of your Affairs:"

"The Lady you Love, has a Gentleman who loves her as violently as you, only a more honourable way: Your Highness's Fortune has altogether the ascendant over his, if you are inclined to lay hold of that advantage, if not, my Art tells me, that, within a Week, she will be too far off for you to enjoy, or ever to see her again."

"And is this all the hopes you can give me? *(said the Prince)*"

"Yes," *(said she)* "only thus much I may add, that your Fortune promises you a great deal of happiness, if ever you have her; but if you Love, I need not tell you this, for Love injoy'd is always happy; since, if there be such a thing as happiness, it is to be in that condition which is most delightful to us; being in possession of what we Love, is being in the condition which is most delightful to us, and thence may well pretend to be the highest of Enjoyments."

"I see you are so indulgent" *(said the Prince)* "as to humour me in my Love, but that is destructive to me, and therefore we'll talk of it no more; there's something *(said he)* by way of gratification, for the trouble I have put you to:"

The *Indian* told him, she would not receive any such reward, for the unwelcome news she had brought him; that all the requital she desired, was his Highness's favour to the *Spaniard*, if ever she found him: Only desired his Highness to take her advice, never to put himself to the trouble, of another attempt on his Mistress, unless 'twas with a design of Marriage, for her Art declared it would prove unsuccessful: That if his Highness ever wanted her help in this, or any other business, he might find her in this Town, where she resolved to stay, till the Army was marched through it to *Limerick*, because that was the likeliest way to find out her Lover.

With these words she took her leave, and taking her Companion with her, left the Prince in the greatest distraction of thought imaginable: The assurance which the *Indian* had given him, that he must expect no success, unless in a Vertuous Love, made him resolve to shake off the mean Passion; but all his endeavours were vain; the more he tryed it, the more sensible he grew, how unable he was to perform it:

He advised with *Celadon*, and they agreed to carry on the Intrigue, in spight of what the *Indian* foretold; and this agreed best with the Prince's humour, who, though he could not entertain the thoughts of Marrying her, could less endure the thoughts of losing her.

They contrived to have it thought about Town, that *Celadon* had fallen into the Prince's displeasure; the Prince shewed the first signs of it in the House, and they of the House soon reported it abroad: *Celadon*, with a seeming discontent, left the prince, and went to Lodge with one of the Officers, at *Marinda*'s Mother's:

There was a young Gentlewoman, a Cousin of *Marinda*'s, and her chief Confident, the same whom the Prince had heard talking with her at the Well, the only comfort of her Parents, who were worth above ten thousand Ducats, of which, their Deaths would leave her the entire Possessour; she was withal very Witty, and good Humoured; but Nature and Fortune, who not often agree to be over-kind to the same person, had here followed their usual Custom, making her want in Beauty, what she had in Riches: And as her Wit was keen, and sharp, upon all that came into her Company, so Nature had given you an exact Copy of her inside, by her out-side; for her Face had as much of Satyr in it, as her Tongue; the Chin of it was sharp and long, the Nose tucked up, as if it fled from her Mouth, which was so wide, as if Nature had designed it for some Cormorant Body: Her Face was all over studded with Freckles, which, like the Stars in the milky way, lay so thick, that you would have thought it one continued yellowness; only her Cheeks, which had a red Colour, but such a tawny one, as that of blasted Goosberries.

This Gentlewoman was then in Town with *Marinda*'s Mother, who was her Aunt, and she was an excellent help to her Cousin, both diverting her from Melancholly with her Company, and helping her with her Advice:

When *Celadon* came to Lodge there, he became acquainted with her; and having remembered, that he once had some discourse with her, while the Prince was entertaining her Cousin, he call'd to mind, how Witty and Pleasant he that time found her Conversation: Their being in the same House, made them often in one anothers Company, and in a little time they grew to a great Familiarity. *Celadon,* hearing what a considerable Fortune she had, made his Addresses to her in earnest, but found her still grow strange, when he spoke to her of that, and therefore thought that something extraordinary was the cause of it: in the mean time the Prince grew reconciled to *Celadon,* and as their falling out, was only a pretence for *Celadon*'s leaving him to Lodge there, so the Prince now made use of that priviledge to his own advantage; for now *Marinda* could no longer avoid him; and though she did as often as she could, yet he came so often thither, that sometimes he lighted on her before she was aware:

Celadon's Chamber was on the same floor with hers, and nothing but a small Gallery divided them; her Chamber was just at the Stair-head, and the Prince would sometimes, as he came up Stairs, find her Door open, and then force himself into her

Company: He this way had frequent access to her, yet could never gain from her the least word in his Favour: In this posture his Amour was, when an Express came to him, that the King had set out of *Dublin*, on his March to *Limerick*; the Prince gave the Officers notice to have all the Souldiers in Arms the next day to receive him:

He went streight to see *Marinda*, because he did not know but the King might take him along with him, as he came through the Town, and so not give him time to take his leave of her: He came into her Mother's, and being used to go often thither to *Celadon*, went up Stairs, without speaking to any body; not seeing her below, he went into her Room, but not finding her there, and seeing her Closet-door open, and a Pen and Ink on the Table, he pulled the Door close, and sat down to write a *Billet Deux*, which he intended to leave for her:

In the mean while *Marinda* came into the Room, and this Cousin with her, and sitting down, they carried on a discourse, the first words of which the Prince did not hear, but the following were to this purpose:

"I tell you, *Marinda*", (*said the Stranger*) "'tis in a happy hour for you, that the King is coming down, for he will take these Souldiers with him, and this Prince, who is so ungentile to endeavour the ruin of a Gentlewoman:"

"I should scarce blame him" (*said* Marinda) "for why should a Man be blamed for prosecuting the way to his own happiness? Nor am I so conceited, as to aim at Marriage; for what private Gentlewoman could nourish such vain hopes as those, of being raised to a Princess? 'Tis more than a bare Prodigy, for Earthquakes, Inundations, and those wonders of Nature do sometimes happen; but that a Prince should marry a private Maid, is such a wonder, as I never found mentioned in all the Chronicles I have read."

"What? Cousin," (*says she*) "and do you plead for him! will you ever consent to his Love on dishonourable terms?"

"No," (*said* Marinda) "as I do his Cause Justice, so I will my own; had not this news of the King's coming prevented me, I would have gone with you to your Father's, to avoid him; now

I will deferr it till I hear the Siege of *Limerick* is over, then I will retire to your House, or some other Relations, where he shall never trouble me again, or I him."

"Ay, do, *Marinda*," (*said her Cousin*) "fly the Tempter: But what shall I do with my Lovers? They are both going to the Camp, and will expect that I give them some satisfactory answer; and I do not know which way to incline; the one is a Captain of Horse, he is approved of by my Father, but disliked by my Mother and me, because he is a Papist, and I have another cause of aversion for him, that is, that he is a Foreigner; I don't fear that all his Country Jealousie can make him suspitious of such a Face as mine; but those on the continent make such saucy domineering Husbands, that no free-born Irish-woman will endure their slavery: There is Celadon a good Humoured, Handsome, Witty Fellow, and one that I like very well; he makes his Courtship so zealously, and swears so seriously that he Loves me, that I do almost believe him; yet the Fellow is so poor, that I fancy neither Father nor Mother will ever consent to my having him; prithee tell me what resolution to take; or whether of the two to favour, my inclination, or my Obedience."

"There is" (*said* Marinda) "come to this Town an *Indian*, who tells Fortunes very true: Shall we" (*said she*) "put on our Masks, and go to her?"

"No," (*said* Marinda) "she will come to me for sending for; I was the first that received her in this Town, and wellcom'd her as a Stranger, and therefore she is very intimate with me:"

"Then pray" (said the Stranger) "let us send for her immediately":

"'Tis not a fit time" (*said* Marinda) "but in the Afternoon I will send her a Message by my Maid, and she shall bring her with her; but we are summoned, here's a Servant come to call us to Dinner."

They went down together, and the Prince stole softly to *Celadon*'s Room, and finding him within, bade him come along with him to his Lodgings; and he bearing the Prince company out, no body suspected, but he had all the while been in *Celadon*'s Chamber. As the Prince walked towards his Lodgings, he told Celadon of his lying hid in the Closet, and all that he over-heard them saying.

"And now Celadon," (*said he*) "what think you of my Condition?"

"What should I think," (*answered* Celadon) "but that you are happy? for you love and are beloved:"

"But what good will that Love do me" (*reply'd he*) "since 'twill never avail me any farther than the bare acknowledgment? Nay, that she Loves me is rather my unhappiness, for did she not, perhaps she would continue here, and I might have those smaller satisfactions, the sight of her, and her Conversation: And I would rather have her Company, though she tortur'd me with disdain, than lose her by this effect of her Love."

"Your Highness" (*said* Celadon) "has better Politicks in War than in Love; if in the Battel your Enemy should fly, would you grieve that he did not stand longer, does not his fight do better? If she had strength enough to resist she'd stand; but she, like him, in her flight confesses her weakness, and in retiring before you does seem to say, '*Come follow me, and Conquer.*' Your Highness saw her Cousin, my Mistress, though her Face is very ordinary, yet her Shape is handsome; she has a very taking Wit, and I hear she has a Bag of Money would blind one sooner, than the most dazling Beauty:"

"And (as I am a Souldier) though I have a great devoir for all the Beauties of the fairer Sex, yet, to my thinking, rich Jewels out-shine the brightest Eyes, and the yellow of the *Leuidores* is a more glorious colour, than the fairest White and Red, that ever made Lover doat, or poet Rhime: I am glad they will send to the *Indian*, for I'll tell them their Fortunes, and order them too, but so much to our advantage, that you shall have your Mistress, and I mine; the way I will go about it shall be this: Your Highness may desire your Landladies pretty Niece to take her Maid with her, and go to the *Indian* to know her Fortune, let her order the Maid in the mean time to stay at the Door, and when the Servant comes from *Marinda*, let her pretend to be the *Indian*'s Servant, and to carry the message up Stairs; let her bring the Servant down word, that her Mistress, the *Indian*, is busie with Company, but will wait upon her Lady in the Evening; then let the young Gentlewoman gratify the *Indian* well for telling her Fortune, and tell her that she has a mind to have a Frollick that Night, and desire the Indian to lend her one of her *Spanish* Suits to Masquerade in:

"When she has brought this Suit home, I will put it on, and go to *Marinda*'s at the appointed time; I will personate the *Indian*, my feigned Voice is shrill enough to pass for a Womans, you know I have got a Foreign tone, as well as she, my height and shape are much the same, and for my Face 'tis no matter, she always wears a Veil, so will I, and as to her gift of Fortune-telling, let me alone to tickle their Fancies."

The Prince was mightily pleas'd with the Stratagem, and said, *Go on and prosper, thou cunning* Proteus,[74] *and may* Celadon *the Prophetess have better luck than* Celadon *the* Franciscan.

The Prince sent up for the young Gentlewoman, and telling her that there was an *Indian* come to Town, who shewed none but Gentry their Fortunes, he desired her to go this Afternoon to ask hers; and told her, that she must borrow a *Spanish* Suit of the *Indian*, as for her self: He gave her a Purse of Gold to pay the expence, and leave as a pawn for the Cloaths, in case the *Indian*, not knowing her, should be unwilling to venture them without Security.

The young Gentlewoman took her Maid with her, and did her business as successfully as they could wish: She had her Fortune told, and the Prince, to whom formerly she made the whole Relation of her Amour, was desirous to know what the event of it would be.

She told him, that the *Indian*, smiling, delivered it in these words; *Be Constant, and be Happy."*

"Thank your kind Fortune", Madam, (said the Prince) "how many a Lover would be over-joy'd at such a Prediction!"

He spake this with a particular earnestness: The Fair Virgin gave the Prince thanks, for sending her to know it, and took her leave of him, not without observing something extraordinary in his Countenance, by which she guess'd that the impartial God of Love, has no more respect for Persons of Quality, than for their Inferiours.

Celadon fell to shifting himself, and having put on the Indian's Habit, looked so like her, that the Prince promised himself both Diversion and Success from this adventure. *Celadon* staid till it grew duskish, because the Night would help the disguise; about an hour after he came back again, and gave the Prince this account of his Success.

"I have been at *Marinda*'s, she took me into the Closet (where you was) very cautiously, lest any one should hear but her Cousin and me, not dreaming who she confessed her self to: She told me that she did Love you, and yet must dissemble it; that she heard your Highness had been in the House, and she thought 'twas to see her; that she expected you would come to take your leave of her, and did not know how she ought to receive you: She said that I told her at first, that she should have you, but now desired me to confess freely, whether I spoke truth then, or did it to flatter her humour; for if it were so, she would not indulge her self the sight of you any more, but wean her self from you for altogether. I found by this, that the *Indian* had soothed her up with the hopes of your Marrying her; I humoured her too, and bade her hope the best: For had I done contrary, that would have contradicted what the *Indian* told her, and given her some grounds to suspect me for a Cheat; besides, despair might have made her refrain your Company for ever: She sighed, and said, she would ask my Advice, whenever she had occasion for it.

"Then her pert Cousin took me up, telling me much the same story that you over-heard her in, and desired to know which of these Lovers she should have: Your Highness may imagine I gave the Verdict on my own side: And after threatening her with all the ill fortune, that can be in the other Servant, I promised her as much happiness in my self; and was so large in my own praises, that it made me blush, under my Veil, while I uttered them. She proffered me a reward for what Advice I gave her, yet would not tell me whether she would take it or no."

"But when I had parted with them, and thought the Joke was over, the pleasantest part of it was to come; for at the Door I met a pretty young Lady, who was come to pay a visit to *Marinda*: 'I was at the Ball; (*says she*) 'when you professed the faculty you have, in fore-telling Events, and now I have met you in a private House, I must needs make tryal of it'; saying this, she took me aside, and having conjured me Secresie, she told me, that she lived in *Dublin*, and was ardently sollicited by one K―――k, a great Officer, in the Army; that he made her vast promises of kindness and everlasting Affection; and she desired to know whether he would prove Constant, if she trusted him:

"After having looked fixedly on her Face, and the palms of her Hands, and used those impertinent Formalities, that your pretended Fortune-tellers do, I bade her never doubt it, my Life for it he would prove true. She could not conceal the Joy she conceived, at my favourable answer; and for my good news, and to bribe me to Secrecy, she clapp'd a *Jacobus*[75] into my Hand. I hope your Highness will not blame me, for cozening the poor Maid, for I thought it might prove my own case another time, to desire one to have the same good Opinion of me, and therefore I thought I ought to do, as I would be done by."

"In the Street I was stopped again, by a spruce Servant Maid, who making a low Curtesie or two, desired me to look in her Hand, and give her a proof of my Skill; she brought me into a Kitchen, to a light, and shewed me her Hand, but begg'd me to be secret, because it concerned her Reputation: I told her, she might speak freely to one who knew not her Name, nor was ever likely to see her again. 'I am Courted' (*said she*) 'by an Old Man, who is very Rich; I love a Young one, who is very poor: The Young one I dare not marry, for fear of Beggery; the Old one I must not, because I cannot endure him: In this uncertainty I would live as I am, were it not that the young Man took his advantage of me in the Critical minute; and now I must make choice of one, or the other, for fear of being with Child, and for ever disgraced; tell me, in this case, which will thrive best with me.' I remember'd I was *Celadon* still, for all my Habit, and therefore considering the necessities of those Youths, whose niggardly Fortune would not let them Marry, and the Dotage of feeble old Age, that will needs be Lovers, when their season's past, I advised her to Marry the Old Man, and keep the Young one; that way (*said I*) you will enjoy the Love of the one and the Riches of the other."

"Her Master coming in at that time, and asking what I was, the Maid told him, I was a Fortune-teller: 'Go thy ways, Girl,' (*said he*) 'and leave me to speak a word to her': When she was gone, he pulled out a Silver Groat, telling me, I should have that to resolve him a question."

"'Sir, (*said I*) though I sometimes tell the Poor their Fortunes for nothing, yet I never do it to the Rich under half a piece. I am not one of your ignorant rambling Gypsies; I'll tell you your Fortune, as it shall fall out to a Hair':"

"'Well, here's half a Piece for you,' (*said he*) 'if you tell it so exactly, for 'tis a thing of moment: I am about to marry a handsome Girl; the only scruple I have against it, is, that these young Jigglets are so wild, that I fear 'twill be hard to keep her constant; tell me therefore, whether she will be true to me, or no?'

"What Age are you of?" (*said I*).

"But threescore and eight", (*said he*):

"I looked in his Hand, and took his Gold, and told him, that the Virgin would prove as honest to him after Marriage, as she was to her Vertue, before he Weds her. This was a true answer, for I fancied it was his own Maid that he meant, and how honest she was, I knew by her own Confession. I went away laughing at the folly of Covetous old Age, that would throw more Money away, towards the satisfying an impotent desire, than he would willingly have given a Physician, for the saving his Life."

The Prince laugh'd at the pleasant use which *Celadon* had made of his disguise; and they two debated for a while which was the greater weakness, that of the Old Man, to trust his Honour to a Young Woman's Vertue; or that of the Maiden, to trust hers to the Constancy of an Officer. The Prince placed his own Folly in the first rank; and said, it was greater than the other two, to trust all the repose and quiet of his Life, to the rigour of a disdainful Woman; to cringe to one that was beneath him, and submit himself to one, who could not pretend to a higher Match, than one of his Dependants: But when Love took her part, it made him recant all these Reflections, clad the meanness of his passion in a lovelier dress, and made it seem, either no fault at all, or one of the least, the most pardonable of his Life. He commended *Celadon's* discretion, in indulging her the hopes of Marrying him, for fear her Vertue should otherwise have made her shun him.

The next morning word was brought to the Prince, that the King was near the Town: He drew up all his Men, in order to receive his Majesty; and after having kissed his Hand, and discoursed with him, concerning the preparations requisite to the Siege, the Prince came home to put all things in readiness for his next days March: But that which he accounted the chief, was to take his leave of *Marinda*.

He found her alone in her Room; and though she seemed uneasie, yet he constrained her to stay, and hear a long story of his passion; which he set forth in the most prevailing words, accompanied with the most winning Carriage, that Art and Nature, joyned together, could invent. At last he gain'd so much upon her, as that she consented to receive a Letter from him, while he was in the Camp. He came back to *Celadon* with a mixture of Gladness and Sorrow; Gladness at the favour she had granted him, the priviledge of Writing to her; and Sorrow to think that he must purchase that satisfaction at so dear a rate, as the loss of her Company, as long as the Siege should continue.

I will not set down how many of these Fits of Joy and Grief he had, whilst he was in the Camp; neither will I Romance so much, as to write down all the thoughts he had of her, and all the many wise Dialogues he had with himself about her; those the Reader can better imagine, than the Author tell; at least, if he has any of the same Passion the Prince was possessed with: That will make him sympathize exactly with his Highness's thoughts, as two Clocks, well made, keep time with one another.

Thus much I know, that they were so importunate with him, that they could neither be lull'd asleep, by the stillness of the Night, nor diverted by the terrors of the Day: They kept him company continually, followed him even into the Enemies

Trenches, and when Shot of all sorts flew thickest about his Ears, they were neither still'd by the noise of the greater, nor frighten'd away by the small. Among all these thoughts, he did not forget those of writing to her; nor had he been three Weeks away, when calling to him one of his trustiest Servants, he ordered him to take Horse for *Clonmell,* and, with all the privacy imaginable, deliver her this Letter.

To the most Charming

MARINDA

*I*F I could think that Absence would have the same effect on you, it has on me, I should be but too happy: Might I hope that it has lessened your Disdain, as much as it has encreased my Love, I should be over paid for all the restless hours, and melancholly thoughts it has cost me. But this is too good Fortune for me to flatter my self with; nor is it likely, that she who shuns her present Lover, should cherish his memory when absent.

We have block'd your Enemies up, won a Fort from them, and daily gain more ground: And O that I were as certain of Conquering you, as of taking the Town! But you, my lovely stubborn Enemy, hold out against all my endeavours: All the Assaults I make serve but to shew your Obstinacy, and my Weakness, and help to confirm the improbability of my gaining you. Yet Despair it self shall not make me give over; but like a resolute General, who will rather dye in the Trenches, than rise from before the Town which he has once laid Siege to; so after all your Repulses, my worst of Fortune shall but make me dye at her Feet, whose Heart I could never gain entrance to.

But do not rashly resolve on my Ruin, but consider, my Lovely Princess, whether it is not juster for your Pity to indulge that Passion, which your Disdain cannot destroy: And so instead of proving the death of your Lover, give him his Life, in letting him live to be

Yours,

S———g.

The Prince awaited the return of his Messenger with a great deal of Impatiency: The next Evening, as he came from an Assault, his Man came to him; and having told his Highness that he had performed his Message to *Marinda*, he gave the Prince a Letter from her, which he opened, after kissing the Seal, and, with a great deal of Pleasure, read these words.

To the Prince of S ——— g.

WHen I received the Honour of a Letter from your Highness, I was in a great strait, whether to return an Answer to it or no: If I did, I thought it would look like Presumption; if not, like Incivility: In this hard choice I thought it best to err on the kinder side, and rather incurr the censure of Rudeness, than that of Ingratitude. How little I am guilty of the latter, your Highness too well knows, by being witness to a discourse, which I never design'd for your Ears; but since it came to them, I cannot recant it.

And though your Highness talks of despairing to take the Town, I can't think you should, when you know how much you have gain'd of it already: But your Highness deals harder with this, than you do with Limerick; you'll offer no Conditions, because you expect it will surrender upon Discretion; you hope that in vain: for though a Traitor within takes your part, and all the cunning you have assaults it from without, yet these ways will not render your Highness Master of this Fort, which will never yield, but upon Honourable Terms.*

Your Highness's

Most humble Servant,
Marinda.

The meaning of this Letter was too plain, to have any false Constructions made upon it; and the Prince, who saw that he must retire, or engage too far, had now a greater conflict with his thoughts, than he had before with the Coyness of his Mistress, he was so equally divided betwixt Love and Interest, that they governed his breast by turns, sometimes one having the better, and sometimes the other. He thought, however, that so kind a Letter as this seemed to require an answer; and therefore, upon the Army's taking the *Irish-Town*, supposing that a little more time would render the King Master of *Limerick*, he wrote her this answer, to prepare him a kind Reception, when the Camp should break up.

TO THE
Most Charming *Marinda*.

AS our taking the Irish-Town *has prepared our way towards the taking of* Limerick, *so I hope the Surrendry of* Limerick *will prepare mine, towards the taking that which I value above all the Cities of the Universe, my Lovely* Marinda; *and my hopes will be mightily cross'd if one Month does not put me in possession both of that and her: She shall then see how much better conditions we'll give her, than we do to our Enemies; when we shall make them accept of what Terms the Conquerour pleases to impose; but my Beautious Fortress, even when she has Surrender'd, shall chuse her own Conditions, and impose what Laws she pleases on her Conquerour: Since, as he receives that Title only from her Favours, so will he any time exchange it, for that of the*

Humblest of her Servants,

S ——— g.

In this Letter, the Prince spake what he truly thought, that *Limerick* would soon be taken; for the King had sent for some heavy Cannon to the Camp, to throw down the walls, and a breach once made, there were thousands of *English* bold enough to have dared all the Enemies Shot, and force their way into the Town, in spite of all the resistance: But Fortune had otherwise ordered it, for *Sarsfeild* with an unusual Bravery, marched with a small Body of Horse, farther into that part of the Country which was Subjected to the *English* Power, than they suspected he durst; surprized the Convoy, and cutting them to pieces, burnt them, their Carriages and Provisions, (which they brought for the Army) to ashes; some of the Carriages he nailed up, and burst the rest; and the Army wanting them to batter the walls, and the hasty approach of the Winter, not giving them time to send for others, they raised the Siege; his Majesty went for *England*; his Forces retired to their winter Quarters, and our Prince to his Mistress.

I trust, the Reader will not think it prejudicial to our Prince's Honour, to come back without taking the Town, this was not his fault, but his Fortunes; the days of Errantry are past, nor have our Warriors now, such Swords as those Knights of old, that could hew a way through the thickest walls, and do wonders greater than our Age will believe: Our Prince did not pretend to impossible Exploits, but as far as pure Natural Force and Courage could go; he might have been ranked in the first File of the Army; he was not ashamed, that he could not do impossibilities, but came back to *Clonmell* with as brisk a Look, and as glad a Heart, as if he had Routed *Sarsfeild*,[78] and laid *Limerick* in Ashes.

The place where he Lodg'd before, was made ready for him, but he had other designs, and therefore Complemented some of the other Officers with those Quarters, and chose *Marinda*'s Mothers for his. But when he first accosted his long absent Mistress, 'twas in Terms so passionate, that the inability of the Author makes him forbear to express them; nor could he match them, though he borrowed *Apollo*'s Brain to invent, and a Quill plucked from one of Cupid's Wings to write them down; neither would he think it safe to express them to the Life if he could, lest a Passion so well represented might prove infectious to those that Read it; and such Charming Words like those in Magical

Books, might raise a Spirit in some Fair Reader's Mind, some rampant Spirit, that would make the Raiser his prey, before she would be able to lay him again: Thus much the Author will assure you, that they had as powerful an effect, as he could desire over his Mistress; or as the most Amorous of my Readers could wish to have over his own:

She laid aside that reservedness which she observed to other Men, and confessed her Love, as freely as she gave it him; that Night, he told *Celadon* of the welcome he received; and *Celadon* asked him, whether he intended to Marry her? This Question put the Prince to a stand, and he asked *Celadon* whether there was any possibility of Enjoying her without it: *Celadon* told his Highness, he would try, and acquainted him with the way, and the Prince approving of it, the next afternoon he put it in Execution:

He went to wait on *Marinda*'s Cousin, whom he Courted, and they two being pretty Familiar, the young Gentlewoman began to talk about the Love the Prince bare her Cousin; she did it to sound him, and to find whether the Prince's Affection was real. *Celadon*, who watched for such an opportunity, said, yes truly, the Prince had an unfeigned Affection for her fair Cousin, so violent a one, that notwithstanding the difference of Quality, the Prince would Marry her if he were single.

"What, is he Married then?" said the young Lady, extreamly surpriz'd.

"Why, did not you know it, Madam?" *said he*. "since through inadvertency I have blabb'd it out, for Heaven's sake do not let it be known that it came from me, for then I shall be for ever out of the Prince's favour."

She promised she would not, and so left him, to carry the News of it with all speed to her Cousin.

The Prince having left a great part of his Men in *Clonmell*, was gone out of Town that Morning at the Head of the rest, accompanying the gross of the Army which was marching towards *Dublin*; and on the morrow about mid-day, he took leave of the Officers, to return to *Clonmell*; he brought but one Man back to wait on him, who had a Horseman's usual Arms, Sword and

Pistols, and the Prince had a slight Morion[79] on, and a Buff-coat, both which he wore, rather for the solemnity sake, (because he went with the Army) than for any use he suspected he should have of them:

Riding along, they came to diversity of Roads; where he and his Man being both Strangers to the Country, lost their way, nor could they meet with any one to direct them into it, only the Voice of some body in a wood just before them; when they drew nearer, they heard the shrieks as of one in distress, and the Prince Riding up, overtook his Man, and put on as hard as he could to see what it meaned; coming nigh, he saw by a Hedge side two Men, who had defended a gap, against twelve, one of them was fallen, and block'd up that place in his Death, which he maintained whilst alive; but was not unrevenged, for two were killed on the other side, and the other Person stood armed with Anger and Despair, and with more Courage than Hopes, maintained the Combat against so unequal a number; the single Person seemed by his Garb to be a Gentleman, he had only a half-pike, which he managed so actively, that with it, he kept off a row of pitch-forks and Swords, which assaulted him; behind him, stood a Lady and her Maid, crying out at every thrust they made at him, and calling upon Heaven and Earth for assistance, against those barbarous Enemies:

The Prince rode up, and commanded them to desist, and let him know what was the cause of their Quarrel; one of them gave him a short Answer in *Irish*, and at the same time made a thrust at him with his Pitch-fork, which by the Prince's sudden spurring his Horse missed him, and ran the Beast into the belly, the Prince drawing out a Pistol, returned the *Irishman*'s Complement with a shot, and laid him dead at his Horse's feet; he had done the same service with his other Pistol, but that Beast enraged with the double wound which *Teague*'s[80] weapon had given him, kick'd and flung so, that the Prince was forced to alight; the Man which waited on his Highness, did more Execution with his Pistols, and having with them, killed one, and wounded another, he alighted and drew his Sword to Fight by his Master, who by this time had dispatch'd two more, not without receiving a great wound, which one of them with a half-pike had given him in the side; the Prince enrag'd at that fell fiercer on the rest, and the Stranger who hitherto had been only on the defensive part, having but one to deal with, gave him his *mittimus*[81] to the other World, and came up to fall on those who had more than their hands-full of the Prince and his Man; but at his coming, finding themselves too weak, they sought that safety in their heels, which their Swords could not give them; the Prince and his Man had Jackboots on, and were unable to follow them; and the Stranger was so weary with the Blood he had lost, and the weariness of so tedious a conflict, that he had scarce strength enough to keep him on his Legs; however, he used that little he had in coming up to the Prince, and thanking him for his own Life, and his beautious Companions; the Prince told him, he owed it to his own Valour, and the favour of Heaven, which seldom fails to help the Couragious, especially when they have Justice on their side:

The Prince ordering his Man to look to the strangers Wounds and bind them up, went himself to Compliment the Lady upon her delivery: He found her leaning on her Maid, bewailing the Death of that Stranger who was killed before he came there, but how was he amazed, when looking in her Face he found it to be *Marinda*:

When he first came in to her assistance, her Hoods were over her Face; which was the Reason he did not know her, and the Beavor[82] of his Morion being down was the cause of the like ignorance in her; though he very little expected to meet her there, yet the joy to see her safe, overcame his amazement, and he was about to testifie it, with all the extasie which his Passion raised in him: When she, casting an angry frown at him, said, "I thought, Sir, to have given my Deliverer the greatest thanks for the rescuing yonder Gentleman's Life, and my Honour, from the Hands of these wicked Villains; but since it is to you I must pay them; I must at the same time declare, that I had rather they should have taken my Life, than, forced me to owe it to you; go, leave me to be a prey to them whom thou hast hunted away, for I had rather dye here, bemoaning this poor Gentleman who fell in the defence of my Honour, than take refuge with you, who whilst you defend it from others, endeavour to prey upon it your self."

He answered her very mildly, and would fain have expostulated with her concerning his Innocence, but she sat over the Dead Gentleman bewailing him, and would not hearken, nor answer one word to what he said; the Prince having found her so kind at his last seeing her in *Clonmell*, wondered strangely at this Capricio of his Fortune, and turning away from her, went to the wounded Gentleman, to see whether he could unfold him the Riddle.

He said, all that he knew of it, was, that the Dead Gentleman was a professed Servant to her, as he was to her Cousin, and that *Marinda* having made a sudden resolution to go for *Dublin*. they two proffer'd to accompany her thither; that she would not let them take as much as a Man with them, because she would not have any one know which way they were gone; that she had desir'd them to avoid the High-roads as much as they could, because she had no mind to be known by any who came from *Dublin*-ward; that in this by-road they met those Rapperees,[83] who bade them deliver; that the Gentleman who Courted her, shot at one of them and killed him; that then they all fell upon them two, who had no other way to defend themselves and the two Women, than by letting them go behind them, and they defend that gap, till some others Riding that Road might come to their help; that the Gentleman was killed, as he made a pass at that second Man who lay Dead by him, and that himself, snatching up the Dead Man's half-pike, as being a better defence than his Sword, had held them all in play till he came into his Rescue.

The Ladies expressing so great a resentment against him, made the Stranger curious to know who it was; but the Servant had no sooner informed him that it was the Prince of S————g, but he begged a thousand pardons for the rudeness his ignorance made him commit; and said, that his Highness had acted with a Bravery suitable to his Quality; and that though he never before had the Honour to know him, yet what he had seen his

Highness perform in this little acquaintance, should make him respect him more for his Deserts, than his Title. The Prince had very little relish for all the Praises the Stranger heaped upon him, and only desired him to prevail with the Lady, to go back to *Clonmell* with him. While the Prince's Man went to catch the Horses, the Stranger persuaded *Marinda* to return back with him; and getting all upon the Horses, they rode before, only the Prince got upon his Man's, and the Man on the Dead Gentleman's, and laying the Body before him, they Rode to the next Town; the Gentleman's wounds were slight ones, and needed little Cure, besides rest and a recruit of Blood; therefore he went with *Marinda* the next day to *Clonmell*; but the Prince's wound was large, and had lost him so much Blood, that his Life was in danger.

Marinda the next day sent him a Surgeon, and a Hearse, to carry the Gentleman to *Clonmell*, he was Buried there, and she shewed such an excessive Grief at his Funeral, that no one who knew he Courted her, but thought that she Loved him; the Prince's being wounded came to *Celadon*'s Ears, but he wondered that it was in rescuing *Marinda*, whom he thought all the while to have been at home; he streight took Horse and came to the Prince, and found him very weak, wanting rest, and incapable of taking any:

To hear that his Rival was so bemoaned by *Marinda*, was worse than Poyson to his wounds; to have seen her prefer another before his face; one who was Dead, and insensible of her Kindnesses, before him, who valued them at so high a rate; and to think, that the other, who was but a private Gentleman, was preferr'd by his Mistress, before him and all his Titles, raised a Noble Indignation in him, which bespread his Face with a redder dye, than that of his Wound. When he had told *Celadon* her unkind Behaviour towards him; he guessed immediately what was the Reason of it, but would not tell the Prince, for fear it should incense him: He only made a slight matter of it, and told his Highness that if he woold write a Line by him, for a pretence to him to see her, he would soon accommodate the difference; and set him as much in her Favour as ever; the Prince seemed to give but little credit to these hopes, but because he would leave nothing unattempted, ordering that no body should disturb their privacy, he bade *Celadon* write, whilst he dictated him these words.

TO THE

Incensed *Marinda*

IF it be a Fault to have rescued my Fair One from her Enemies; if it be a Crime unpardonable, to have spent a great part of my Blood in revenging the death of my Rival, because I did not lay down my Life with his, then will I offer up the poor remainder of my Blood, to atone for the Cowardise I have been Guilty of; and shall think my Life sold at too dear a rate, if it should draw so many precious Tears from your Eyes, as did that happy Gentleman, who even in his Death triumphed over the Love of his Survivor.

But if I was as willing to expose my self for your sake, and he was the first in your Defence, only by the good Fortune, of being with you at the beginning of the danger; I know not why the living Servant should not share more of your favour than the dead one; since he would have died as willingly at your Feet, had not your Fortune commanded him to live till he conquered your Enemies. Now he has kept his Life too long, since it is become odious to you, and would gladly lay it down before the Face of his incensed Divinity, if his weakness would permit him to come there: And if he has any desire at all to live, it is only so long till you let him know in what he has offended you: This sure is the least you can grant to one, who was once so happy in your favour; and 'tis all the satisfaction your Criminal desires, to know why you have condemned him, since he has always been the

Faithfullest of your Servants,

S ———— g.

When *Celadon* got to Town, he came streight to *Marinda*'s: She was not to be spoken with, but he met with *Diana*, (so was his Mistress called) and after the usual Complements past, he asked her how he should speak with her Cousin:

"No way," (*said she*) "there's no access for you, because you come from the Prince."

"Why, Madam," *said he*, "is not *Marinda*, satisfied that the Prince has sufficiently hazarded his Life in her defence, but that she'll endanger it farther by her Cruelty?"

"Cruelty!" (*answered she*) "why what kindness can he expect from a Virtuous Woman? Or what would the Wedded S —— g with the Chaste *Marinda*"

"And is that all the reason of her Anger?" (*said* Celadon,) "Has the poor Prince suffered all this for a word of mine? By Heaven (*Madam*) the Prince is single, and I am perswaded has as vertuous designs on your Cousin, as I have on you."

"If he has no more on her" (*answered she*) "than I have on you, he would never again be at the expence of a sigh for her: For your part, I here discharge you my acquaintance; your mischievous Jest has been the cause of a great deal of Grief, both to my Cousin and me, for the Gentleman's death, the other Gentleman's weakness, and the endangering the Prince's Life: You have jested fairly, you had like to have jested the Prince at once out of his Life and Mistress, your-self you have jested out of my Favour, I will assure you; and so farewell good jesting, Mr. *Celadon*, for if I ever any more admit of your Jests, I'll give you leave to make a Jest of me as long as you live."

Saying this she flung away into her Cousins Room, and all that *Celadon* could say, could not get either of them to speak a word to him. She told *Marinda* that the Prince was innocent, and, by *Celadon*'s Confession, had no designs, but what were honourable and virtuous: At the same time the Maid came up, and brought them a Letter, which *Celadon* sent to *Marinda*, and the same which he had written from the Prince's Mouth; the Servant told them that he was returning to the Prince, and desired to see them before he went, that he might know what Service they had to command him. Neither of them would consent to see one who had been the Author of their late troubles: But *Diana* told her Cousin that the Prince, who was innocent, ought not to suffer for him; that she should rather shew her self kinder than ever, to one she had so causelesly tormented: *Marinda*'s own Love did take his part so much, and joyn so prevalently with her Cousin's Arguments, that it made her give some small interval to her Griefs, to pay that which was due to her Love.

She wrote a Letter, and sent it to *Celadon*, who made what haste he could to leave an angry Mistress, to see his wounded Prince, and cure his Body, by this sovereign Ballsom which he brought for his mind. The Prince (when he came before him) would not stay to tell him how he did, till he first asked how he had succeeded.

"As well for you, Sir," (said he) "*as you can wish, and as ill for my self; how ill for my self, I will tell you hereafter; how well for your Highness, this Letter will acquaint you.*"

At these words he gave him the Letter; and the Prince, with a great deal of haste, breaking it open, found these words.

To the Prince of S ———— g.

H*Ow shall I be silent, when Justice obliges me to confess I have wronged you? Or how shall I have the face to confess a Rudeness, which a misunderstanding made me guilty of? I was too rash to condemn you without a hearing'; but I hope your Highness will pardon that rashness, when you shall consider it was in the defence of (that which I prefer before all things) my Vertue. Though the weakness of my Sex makes me careful of my life; yet did your Highness need it, I could willingly expose it as lavishly in your behalf, as you did yours in mine: Yet my Innocence (which is dearer to me than that Life) I must not sacrifice, no, not to you.*

Your Highness has more Generosity, than to begrudge a Gentleman a few tears, who lost his Life in my defence: They were no more than what I owed both to Gratitude and Humanity: Neither ought you to infer from thence, that the Dead shares more of my Favour than the Living: I would convince you of the contrary, if it were fitting: But your Highness's condescention must not make me forget, that you are a Prince, and that my highest deserts rise no higher than to be the

Humblest of your Servants,
Marinda.

"You deserve all things, Divine *Marinda*," (*said the passionate Prince*) "what Title is too High, or Estate too Magnificent to admit you for a Partner? I will no more indulge this vain Ambition, or let it cross my Love: Tell me, *Celadon*," (*said he*) "does not *Marinda*, with her natural Beauty look finer than our Proudest Court Ladies, tho' decked with all their Gaudy Costly Dresses? Yet that lovely Body is but the Shell of a more glorious Inhabitant, and is as far out-shone by that more radiant Gust,[84] which lies within, as your choicest Jewels exceed the lustre of the Cask, which holds them: For her Illustrious mind has got as inexhaustible a store of rare perfections in it, as the famed *Potosi*[85] has of Riches: And as in that the greedy *Spanish* Conquerour, the farther he diggs, finds still more new supplies of Ore; so whoever makes himself Master of her richer Heart, will still discover there new Mines of Radiant Vertues, so infinite they are, that they would tire the most inquisitive Lover to find them all, and each of them has such peculiar Charms in't, enough to make him leave his scrutiny after more, to admire that one which his first search does find."

"Ah, Sir," (*said* Celadon,) "now your Highness is happy and in favour, you do not consider him who is clearly cast off by his Mistress, for what he did only with design to serve you; for it was my telling *Diana* that your Highness was married, and confessing the falshood afterward, has so put me out of her favour, that she has forbidden me ever seeing her again."

"Tho'" (*said the Prince*) "that was an unlucky Policy of yours, yet since 'twas well designed, you shall not suffer for it, and therefore take my word, that the same day which makes my happy, shall make you so to; and as our Loves are joyn'd, so shall our Fortunes."

"Your Highness" (*said* Celadon) "cannot be more in Love with the perfections of your Mistress, than I can with the Wit and good Humour of mine: Besides, her Baggs which are so large and tempting, it would grieve my heart to part with them, after I was in so fair a way for obtaining her."

The Prince answered, that both their Loves waited only for his Health, and then he would soon see them consumated. He wrote two or three Letters more to *Marinda* whilst he lay ill, but the reader must excuse me, if I produce them not here, since *Marinda* burned them to prevent a discovery; and Secretary *Celadon* was not so careful to keep any Copies.

Now had the active Sun run through our Celestial sign, and his pale Sister gone through her Monthly course, and changed her Orb, whilst the poor Prince kept his Bed, and with the loss of Blood had been as pale as she; at length the help of Art restored his Health, strengthning nature began to exert her power, and tho' she was not risen of a sudden to her former vigour, yet she made great advances, and every day perceived her strength encreasing:

His impatient Love would stay no longer than till he was able to travel, and then it carried him back to *Clonmell*, to see his long absent Mistress: He rode to his Lodgings at *Marinda*'s Mothers, but hearing Musick in the House, and the Mirth of Company within, he asked what was the Matter.

"'Tis," (*said one*) "a preparation for Madam *Diana*'s Wedding, who is just now to be Married."

"Married!" *said* Celadon, "O that I had either come sooner or later; for my Honour sake I cannot see my Mistress Married away before my Face, and yet I am come too late to prevent it; but what can be done on such a sudden I'll do." Saying this, he alighted, and rushed into the House, and the Prince followed him in to see what his design was.

Celadon entered just as the Ceremony began, and with a threatening voice cryed, "*I forbid the Banes; and if the intended Bridegroom will defer his hopes so long, to go aside with me, I will convince him, that my Title to her is better than his.*"

The Company wonder'd to see this Challenge laid to her; her Relations, who were by, expected her to speak; but she was prevented by the Bridegroom, who fiercely cryed, that it belonged to none but him, to vindicate his Title to her: Some

Officers were there, the Bridegrooms Friends, and would have taken up his quarrel, but forbore out of respect to the Prince, expecting what he would do in it. The Prince knowing the Gentleman to be the same whom he had seen Combat with so many Enemies, to save *Marinda*, had such an opinion of his Valour, that he would fain have decided the Quarrel, without injuring either of the Pretenders: Had she been at his disposal, *Celadon* should have had her, if at her Parents, they had decided it for the *Spaniard*: Therefore he thought it best to leave it to her self, and therefore spoke to this purpose.

"*Gentlemen, I have such an esteem for you both, that I would not have you fight, since, which ever falls, the Law will lay hold on the other, and so in striving which shall have the Lady, both of you will lose her; if you will stand to my advice, let it be thus. Refer your Cause to the Lady, and give her three days time to consider of it, in which time let both of you have free access to make your Court to her, and at the three days end, let her take which she will: If,* Celadon, *her choice does decide it, against you, you must submit; but if she like you best, there is no reason why your staying with me in my illness, should make you lose your Mistress.*"

The Gentleman said, that, since he owed his Life to the Prince's Valour, he would not deny him this; and *Celadon* was glad to win so much to try his Fortune in. While the three days lasted, the two Suiters took their turns to Court *Diana*:

On the fourth day, the Musick play'd again, the Priest was present, and the admiring Company stood in suspence, to see who was the destined Bridegroom. The Bride stood out, and in making her Choice, spake thus:

"*You are here come together, my Relations, and good Acquaintance, to see me Married, and I am happy in having the choice of two Gentleman, the refused of which may, if his deserts are answered, have many a better proffer; however, if they were ever so good, one of them must be rejected, therefore I would not have the disappointed one take it ill that I refuse him.*

"*One of them has been longer my Servant, but the other was more zealous while he was so: The Spaniard has been the more Complaisant, but the* Englishman *the Fonder: The* Spaniard *the truer Courtier, but the* Englishman *the truer Lover; therefore, as commonly Love is soonest raised in one Breast, by seeing it first in the other, so the* Englishman *has the advantage of the* Spaniard, *and my heart catched that Passion, as it were by Contagion from his: Yet, on the other side, I should not forget my Duty; my Father takes the* Spaniard's *part, well, but Love takes the* Englishman's: *Then I must beg my Father's pardon, if I leave the* Spaniard *to receive his reward from him whom he courted, and desire the Company to judge, if I ought not rather to yield him my Love, who sued to me for it, than to him who Courted my Parents."*

The Company was divided in their opinions, as their Acquaintance byassed them; and some murmured at the Inconstancy of her Humour, whilst others applauded her Choice. *Celadon* ran to give her thanks, with all the kindest expressions his Joy could inspire him with; and his Rival, distracted with Grief and Shame at his unexpected repulse, stood uncertain on that sudden Emergency, how to behave himself:

He was awaked out of this Trance, by a Gentlewoman, who came to him, and said, "Take heart, Seignior, be not ashamed of a Denial, which not your want of merit, but my Contrivance was the occasion of; 'twas I that persuaded the Lady to refuse you, and I trust you will pardon me, when I say it was for my own sake that I did it."

Without question the Company thought this an odd sort of Confidence, for a Gentlewoman to Court a Man, in so kind terms, and so publickly too: Her Garb was very fine, her Shape and Air gentile, and her Face, which was one of the most amiable ones there, spake her to be in the prime if her years; yet neither her Dress, Youth, Beauty, or Love, could prevail the least on our discontented *Spaniard*, who would not once vouchsafe to look on her.

"What then," (*said she*) "is my Constancy thus requited? Or can two years time cause so much alteration, as to make *Astolfo* forget me?"

These words made the *Spaniard* turn towards her, and he no sooner saw her Face, but he cry'd out, "am I in a Dream? Or do I truly behold once again, the Face of my beloved *Faniaca*? Now,

Celadon, I yield thee up thy Mistress, and quit all my pretensions to her, for this which I have newly found." *Celadon* gladly thanked him for his submission to *Diana's* Choice, and all the Company bore a part with the *Spaniard* in the Joy he conceived at the change of his Mistress:

But the beautiful *Indian*, who longed to hear how he came for *Ireland*, said, "It is now, my *Astolfo*, two years since you and I parted, wonder not then if I am desirous to know what befell you since that, and how you escaped a Death which so apparently threatened you; my endeavours to find you out here, made me relate all the passages of our Acquaintance hitherto, and therefore I believe there is no accident in the remaining part of your Life, which is too secret for the Ears of this honourable Company:"

"I have had none", (*said he*) "which I will not freely tell, but to the understanding my Relation, it is requisite that this Illustrious Company should know some things, which for want of opportunity, have as yet been a secret to you, as well as to them.

"My Father is a Gentleman of a plentiful Estate near *Sevill*, by my Mothers death he was left a Widdower with two Children, Me and a Daughter, both which he was very fond of, as being his only Comforts, the Relicts of his deceased Wife, and the Pledges of his youthful Love: There lived near us an old Couple who had the like number of Children, a Son and a Daughter, they were intimate Friends of my Father's, and so free with us, that notwithstanding the severe restraints of our Countrey upon young Persons, yet our Families observed no such Custom, but we young ones conversed with one another with the same freedom as if we had been near Relations:

"And as youthful familiarity in different Sexes, usually ends in Love, so it proved with us, for our Neighbour's Son and my Sister had such a mutual Affection, that they were never well but in one anothers Company; and his Sister, whether by her own inclination, or their setting on, seemed as uneasie unless when she was in mine; had she been handsome, perhaps I should have taken as much diversion in his Sister's Company, as he did in mine; but I thought those Complements thrown away, which were bestowed on an ugly Face; nor could my Wit help me with one fond Vow or happy Expression, for want of Beauty to inspire it:

"This made me avoid her Company to get into his; but when I saw him shun mine as much, and that he and my Sister coveted to be always together; his growing more reserved to me than formerly, and some symptoms which I perceived in my Sister; her frequent sighs at parting, her blushes at meeting him, and some other slips, which the most dissembling of your Sex find difficult to hide, gave me apparent cause to think that she loved him.

"He and I were once as great as 2 *Brothers* laid our breasts open to one another thence his never discovering the least to me, concerning his passion for my Sister, made his Love look to me, as if it designed nothing that was honest.

"I had then to wait on me a *Turkish* Captive, who was taken away young, and having been bred up several years in my Father's House, was very trusty and discreet; I let no one know my suspitions, but him, and ordered him to be a Spy on all my Sister's Actions; and if ever he observed any thing remarkable between them two, that he would acquaint me with it: He observed my Commands, and one time brought me word, that he had over-heard him and my Sister discoursing; that she desired him to ask her of my Father, and that very soon, or she should be discovered to be with Child, and so be disgraced, and turned out of Doors; tho' this was but what I feared to find out, yet now I found those fears true, it enraged me both against him and my Sister:

"However, the consideration of her Sex's weakness (which is an unequal Combatant for Love, when assisted by earnestness and opportunity) made me pardon her so far, as to leave her to be punished by the ill consequences of her own Folly; but him I resolved to be revenged on:

"Tho' my blood boyled at the first sight of him, yet I dissembled my anger in publick, and told him that I had something to impart to him, if he would take a walk with me into the Fields in the cool of the Evening; he consented, and we went out together; as we walked on talking, I drew him insensibly to a private place, and then retiring a little distance from him, I bade him draw:

"'Sure you are in jest' (*said he*) 'you will not draw that Sword against your Friend, which you have before now drawn in my defence:'

"'This Sword' (*said I*) 'was drawn then for my Friend, but now against the worst of mine Enemies, one who has abused my Friendship, and my Sister's Love: Yet thus much I will give to our former Affection, Marry her, and salve up the injury thou hast done her, and I will forgive thee mine':

"'What,' (*said he*) 'and are you turned a Bravo to hector me into Marriage? Know then that I will never do it, neither shall it ever be said, that *Guzman* valued his Honour so little, as to make a Wife of his Whore.'

"'Whore!' (*said I*) 'that word I will engrave on thy traiterous Heart'";

"at these words he leapt back and drew, I made at him with a great deal of Fury; but being appeased by some Blood I drew from him, I proffered him again the same conditions of Reconciliation; but his Rage made him deaf to Reason: We fought on, till one thrust I made at his Breast ended our difference, by his fall:

"I fled in all haste to the Sea-side, where by good chance there was a Ship under Sail bound for the *Indies*; I went aboard her; Landed in *America* amongst some Souldiers, who were sent to re-inforce our Country Garrisons there: I was a private Souldier, till a Fight that I signalized my self in, raised me to a Captain's Commission; 'twas in this station I was, when I came acquainted with you: You know the Captain of the Man of War, which boarded us, sent me Prisoner to *Sevill*, with my other Countrymen:

"Near this Town my Father lived; I sent him word of my being in Prison, and he streight came to see me, but told me, he must not own me for his Son, lest it should cost me my Life: He applauded my revenging the dishonour done to my Family; but said, that there had been Warrants issued out against me, and

500 Duckats, by the deceased's Friends, promised him that should seize me; that if I should stand a Tryal, and escape the Law, yet their private revenge would reach me; therefore, he said he would make Friends for me and my fellow Prisoners, that we should be dismissed, and then he would have me spend some years abroad, and when Time, or Death had cured the malice of my *Enemies*, he would get my pardon, and call me home.

"I took his advice, and as soon as I was freed, hearing that the *Hollanders* were raising Souldiers, for some design they had not yet divulged, I entered Volunteer into that Party which came for *England*; you have all heard how we succeeded, and that instead of a Battel, we came as it were to a Triumph; for the *English* came over to our side; thence we took Shipping for *Ireland*, and in *Dublin* I received a supply from my Father, which bought me the Command of a Troop; I was at the *Boyn* near *Schomberg*[86] when he was killed; I lay in the Camp before *Limerick*, and took my chance of War, among those Brave Men that fell in the Trenches; I Quarrelled with the Prince t'other Night, mistaking him for some Rival that Serenaded *Diana*; but the Guards coming up, and my finding out my Errour, delivered me from his Sword too:

"I was afterwards engaged with ten *Irish* at once, and fortunately rescued by the Prince's Valour; so that my kind Stars preserved me through all these dangers, to fall the second time a Victim to your Eyes, my former Conquerours; I Courted I confess that Lady, but it was, because I saw not the least likelihood, of ever finding my Beloved *Faniaca*, and therefore, I thought her Fortune would prove a good shelter for a Banished Man, who had been tossed from *Spain* to the *Indies*, from the *Indies* to *Spain*, from *Spain* to *England*, from *England* hither, and one, that durst not set foot again on his Native Country:

"Besides her Wit and good Humour, placed her much in my Esteem, though all those Perfections vanish in any Woman, when you my incomparable Mistress are by."

Thus the *Spaniard* ended his Relation, and the Company with no little pleasure, reflected on the alterations of Fortune; which, after tossing them so far asunder, by the contrary gusts of Adversity, now by one prosperous Gale, brought them together to their desired Harbour:

The two Happy Couples would willingly have prevented all future dangers, by fastning that indissoluble Knot, which nothing but Death can untye, but *Marinda* desired her Cousin, to forbear hers for two or three days; and the Fair *Indian* desired her *Spaniard*, to defer their Joys so long, it not being fit, that she should be admitted to so Solemn a Ceremony of the Church, as that of Matrimony, till she were first listed among the number of her Children: The Priest who came there to Celebrate their Marriage, performed this Solemnity, and all the Company wished the Fair Convert Joy: Mirth and Feasting took up the rest of the day, and made up an intire Friendship, between the Brisk *Celadon*, and the Valiant *Spaniard*, who now Quarrelled no longer for a Mistress.

But if some good natured Reader should be too much concerned for the Amorous Prince, whose intrigue seems to have stood still, whilst the others have run almost to the end of their Race; let him know, that his went the same pace with theirs; though the Author, to comply with *Marinda*'s Modesty, brought her not so openly acting the Lover's part, as he did the brisk *Diana*, or the bolder *Indian*; for as the main wheel of a Clock, though it turns all the rest, yet goes it self with such an insensible motion, that to an unskilful Eye it seems to stand still; so the Prince's and *Marinda*'s Amour, was carried on indiscernably to others, and seem'd to them to be at a stand, whilst indeed it was the chief mover of the two other Intrigues, and pointed out to them the long wished for, the Matrimonial Hour: You must therefore understand, that after all the dark unsuccessful days which our Prince had sighed away, in doubtful Hopes, distracting Fears, and his last black ones of Despair; Fortune vindicated her old Title of Inconstancy, in being kind to him again, in bringing him that propitious critical minute, in which they say, the Coyest Lady (if you nick the right time) is to be won:

The Prince exactly hit it in the first Visit he made *Marinda*; as soon as the designed Marriage was deferred, and the Company gone, he went to pay his particular Respects to the Lady of his Vows:

He found her in the Garden with her Cousin, discoursing about the unexpected breaking off her Marriage, and *Celadon* according to his priviledge, taking her into an Ally aside, left the Prince in another, with *Marinda*; and what time they had there together, he improved to the utmost, in shewing her how sincerely he had been her Servant, from the first sight he ever had of her, till then; and told her, what he required of her in retaliation, and upon what Honourable Conditions he expected it; she answered with all the kindness due to so fond a Lover, and with a mixture of that submissive Civility, which she paid him as he was a Prince, tho' one who professed himself her Servant; and that his Highness might not censure her to have been either Rude or Cruel in her Behaviour towards him, through the whole course of their Acquaintance; she desired, that he would hear those things from her Cousin's Mouth, which she thought not so fit for her own; *Diana* was called for, and *Marinda* desiring her to acquaint the Prince with all she knew of her Thoughts, without disguising any thing; she Discoursed with *Celadon* apart, while her Cousin began thus to the Prince, who was more than ordinarily attentive.

"When my Cousin ordered me to tell you her greatest privacies, those of her Love; she did but give the Reins to that passion, which has alwaies been too strong for her, since first the Graces your Highness is master of, reduced her to the condition of a Lover; and I question not, but she has had undeniable proofs of an equal Affection in you; or else, (by what I know of her Humour) she would rather have Died, than once suffered it to be known; your Highness over-hearing our Discourse at the Well, opened a light to the discovery of that Affection, which otherwise had been doom'd to perpetual obscurity; for though your Highness, did make some Addresses to her, which as she told me, served to ruin her the more, yet they would never have proved any advantage to you; since we both thought, that you spoke out of Raillery more than any serious design; besides, in the highest tide of her Passion, she professed, she would rather suffer any thing than own it to you; the first Night your Highness Serenaded her, she shewed so little concern at it, till you were gone, that I thought it had been a Frolick of the *Spaniard*'s Gallantry, who about that time came acquainted with me, 'twas I spoke to you out of the window, though when the difference of Voice discovered my mistake, I broke off the parly; that time the *Indian* came to Town, and lighting first into my Cousin's Acquaintance, she told her the Dream she had about you; I will not tell it over again, because your Highness has heard it already, only in vindication of the *Indian*'s Skill, let me assure your Highness, that she told my Cousin, she should have the Gentleman she Dreamed of; she interpreted the little Archer, who was on your side, to be Love, the Giant on hers, Honour; that Honour's going over to your side, and leaving her defenceless, signified, that your proffering to Marry her, would overcome her obstinacy; and the Cupid's shooting her through, is easie enough to be left to your Highness's Explanation; the *Indian* promising her success, made her indulge that Love, which she bridled before, and brought her abroad to the Ball":

"*Marinda*, Madam, was not at the last Ball," *said the Prince*:

"Yes, Sir," *said* Diana, "if your Highness remembers, there were two in *Spanish* Dress, the one was the *Indian*, the other *Marinda*;"

"but sure," *said the Prince*, "*Marinda* was not with her in my Room the next day":

"She was with your Highness both times," *said* Diana; "nay, it was she whose Advice you asked in the Closet; she came home that Night, with all the marks of a violent Grief, at something which your Highness had said to her, and resolved withall, never to see, hear, or speak to you more; when she represented[87] the Fortune-Teller, she forbad your Highness to prosecute the Intrigue any farther, unless you designed to carry it on Honourably; and your going on with it, by giving her your Company so often afterwards, and the *Indians* still averring that she was destined for you, made her believe, your Highness had altered your mind for the better; as you know, Lovers above all People are aptest to believe things will come to pass fortunately, meerly because they would have it so; this her belief was strengthned by the kind promising Letter you sent her from *Limerick*; which Letter, induced me too, to think that your Highness had designed something to her advantage:

"You saw what a free reception she gave you, at your return from the Camp, till *Celadon*'s telling me that you were Married, dashed all the Joy I conceived at the prosperity of her Amour, and was very near breaking her Heart, in endeavouring to gain a Conquest over her Love; but when she found how difficult that was, she said, she would punish your illegal Passion, and her own at the same time; and lest a fit of Love should make her recant, she put it in Execution immediately; there was a Gentleman of a considerable Fortune, who had seen her at my Father's in *Dublin*, and fallen in Love with her; this Gentleman being then come to *Clonmell* to see her, she desired him to wait on her to *Dublin*, and I desired my Servant the *Spaniard*, that he would accompany her thither; she told me, that she would rather Marry him whom she did not Love, than give a longer encouragement to any unlawful Affection, which your Highness might entertain for her; that would have bereaved you of her for ever, had not she been met by those Rapperees; her Servant fell there, and though she was mightily concerned for your Highness's danger, yet her Vertue drew those Tears from her, which she thought due to her Defender's Misfortune; and might serve to make you despair, ever coming into her Favour again:

"But when *Celadon* undeceived us, by telling me that your being Married, was only an invention of his own, Shame and Love returned very powerfully upon her; Shame, that she had used you so ill without a cause; and that Love, which before was only supprest by her Resentments, flourished now with greater vigour than before:

This discovery which regained your Highness her Affection, lost *Celadon* mine; and my Anger at his crafty deceit, and his being the cause of so much bloodshed, (thought innocently) made me resolve on the same way to get rid of him, which my Cousin designed against you, that is, by Marrying another; and the *Spanish* Gentleman, who had my Father's Consent, coming then wounded from a Journey which he undertook to serve me; I thought once to reward his Service, and punish *Celadon*'s Falseness, and imagined I might do it with less disturbance, whilst your indisposition kept him out of the way; but Fate, which they say presides over our Marriages, as well as our Deaths, ordered it otherwise, and brought him just time enough to suspend it.

The Prince gave the most ample demonstrations of Joy, at the setledness which this Relation shew'd to be in *Marinda*'s Love; and having thank'd the Ingenious *Diana* for the comfort she had given him, he walked towards the other Couple; they joyned Company, and the Prince desired *Marinda* that she would compleat his Happiness, by setting *Celadon* as high in his Mistress's Favour, as himself was in hers:

The Beautiful *Marinda* granted him this request, as the first demonstration of her Obedience; she endeavoured it so effectually, that presently she made her Cousin pardon *Celadon*'s former miscarriage, and receive him again into her favour; neither did *Marinda* find it any thing difficult to persuade her to this; for of all People, Mistresses are the most forgiving, indulgent Persons to those they Love; and let them dissemble it as much as they please, they cannot be long Angry at any fault a Lover commits, unless it seem to proceed from want of Affection; but *Celadon* not being of that Nature, was soon forgiven, and as a proof of it, was encouraged to hope she would Vote for him:

The next morning, the *Indian* came to wait on the two Cousins, and told *Diana*, that he who was in Election to be her Husband, was the *Spaniard* whom she had been so long looking for; *Marinda* had invited her to the Wedding, and she came in a little after the Prince had deferr'd it, and then seeing it put off, would not discover her self to the *Spaniard*; she desired *Diana* to keep him still in ignorance, that when he was refused, she might see how he would excuse himself to her:

Diana desired no less than she, that it might be kept secret, lest *Celadon* should esteem her Love the less, thinking that the

Spaniard being owned by another, made her take him for a shift; this was the result of the three days Tryal, and hence it came to pass, that the *Spaniard* dejected at the loss of one Mistress, was elevated by the unexpected finding out another, whom he Loved better: The short prorogation of their Marriages, only continued till the Prince had prepared for his; at last the expected day came, and rewarded the three longing Lovers with the intire possession of their Mistresses:

The Beautiful *Marinda*, the Ingenious *Diana*, and the Pritty *Faniaca*, submitted themselves to the power of their Youthful Conquerours. *Diana* had all the felicity she could with, in having him she Loved; the *Indian* gained not only her dear *Spaniard*, but a Fortune with him, for he that day received News from his Father, that his old Enemy was Dead, his Pardon taken out, and with it, he had orders to come home, and take possession of an Estate his Father gave him; the Beautiful *Marinda* received the reward of her invincible Vertue, in Loving and being Beloved, and in having gained a Prince, who raised her Quality as high (in comparison of what she was before) as a Woman's Ambition could desire; these were the Pleasures of the Wedding Day, heightned by the addition of Musick, Feasting, and Mirth; but the Night came, we must like their Bride Maids, conduct them to their Beds, and drawing the Curtains leave them there, to the full Enjoyment of those Pleasures, whose Raptures, none but Experienced Lovers know, and the Constant ones may expect to attain.

FINIS

NOTES

[1] Versions of this introduction have appeared in *Durham University Journal*, June, 1985, *Studies*, Summer 1986, and in my book *Novel and Romance* (Macmillan, 1989).
[2] Halkett, Samuel and Laing, John, *A Dictionary of the Anonymous and Pseudonymous Literature of Great Britain*. 4 vols. (Edinburgh, 1882-88).
[3] 4 vols., London, 1910. All further references are to Volume IV of this edition.
[4] p. 416.
[5] *Ibid*.
[6] p. 430.
[7] Waterford, 1907, p. 96.
[8] cf. Nicholas Canny's paper "Industry Formation in Ireland: the Emergence of the Anglo-Irish" in *Colonial Identity in the Atlantic World* 1500-1800 ed. N. Canny, A. Pagden (Princeton, 1987), pp. 159-212.
[9] This does not mean, however, that the settlers had at last come to identify with the native Irish — far from it. They still saw themselves as distinct from the native Irish as from a race of barbarians.
[10] Charlotte Morgan in *The Rise of the Novel of Manners: A Study of English Prose Fiction Between 1600 and 1740* (New York, 1911), did notice and comment on *Vertue Rewarded*, but gives the distinct impression of confusing it with some other work. She describes the heroine Marinda, for instance, as being among the prisoners taken after the battle of the Boyne, (p. 63), a statement, quite at variance with the facts as revealed in the work. Subsequent inaccurate comments by Morgan on *Vertue Rewarded* tend to confirm the impression of confusion on her part.
[11] *The History of the English Novel*. 10 Vols. (London, 1924-1939).
[12] cf. *Novel and Romance: A Documentary Record* (London: 1970), p. 4.
[13] *The Secret History of Queen Zarah and the Zarazians; Being A Looking Glass for   In the Kingdom of Albigion* (London, 1705), preface, no page numbers.

[14] *Ibid.*
[15] From a letter of Philip Stanhope (1740-1741?). Reprinted Williams, *Novel and Romance*, p. 100.
[16] No. 26, Monday, May 14, 1787; reprinted Williams, *Novel and Romance*, p. 341.
[17] *Popular Fiction Before Richardson: Narrative Patterns 1700-1739* (Oxford, 1969), p. 172.
[18] *Ibid.*, pp. 172, 173.
[19] Richettei, *Popular Fiction*, p. 123.
[20] *Ibid.*, p. 125.
[21] *Ibid.*, pp. 148, 152.
[22] *The Adventures of Lindamira. A Lady of Quality* (Minneapolis, 1949), Introd., p. vi.
[23] *Ibid.*, pp. v, vi.
[24] *Popular Fiction*, p. 170.
[25] *Ibid.*, p. 172.
[26] *Ibid.*, pp. 170, 171.
[27] *Ibid.*, p. 171.
[28] *Ibid.*, p. 173.
[29] *The Power of Love: in Seven Novels* (London, 1741), p. 178. Duplicate of 1720 edition, with new title page. All further references are to this edition.
[30] Samuel Richardson, *Pamela*, Everyman's Library Edition, 2 volumes (London: J. M. Dent, 1962), i, 19. All further references are to this edition.
[31] Though one must admit that in each case the title of one narrative and the subtitle of the other, tends to give the game away.
[32] p. 88.
[33] *Pamela*, i, 192, 199; *The Irish Princess*, 33.
[34] *Pamela*, i, 151; *The Irish Princess*, 83 ff.
[35] *Pamela*, i, 164 ff.; *The Irish Princess*, 69, 78 ff., 99.
[36] *Pamela*, i, 29; *The Irish Princess*, 33.
[37] In her dream, Marinda imagines the Prince 'had hidden himself in my Bed-chamber, and, when I came in, started out upon me: He . . . catched me in his Arms, and told me I was his Prisoner, at which methought, I swooned away with a pleasing pain and at the fright of it I awaked' (32).
[38] i, 145, 146.
[39] i, 47 ff. i, 177 ff.
[40] *Pamela*, i, 189 ff. i, 202 ff.; *Vertue Rewarded*, 66, 67, 87.
[41] This latter phrase is very reminiscent of one used by Pamela

when she hears of the bogus marriage Mr B. is about to offer her: 'Here should I have been deluded with the hopes of a happiness that my highest ambition could have aspired to!' (1, 199).
[42] p. xi.
[43] pp. 30 ff, 69 ff.
[44] p. 69.
[45] T. C. D. Eaves and B. D. Kimpel, *Samuel Richardson: A Biography* (Oxford: The Clarendon Press, 1971), p. 584.
[46] *Ibid.*
[47] *Selected Letters,* p. 229.
[48] *Ibid.,* p. 231.
[49] *Ibid.,* p. 39.
[50] *Ibid.,* pp. 39-42.
[51] p. 39.
[52] p. 232.
[53] *Selected Letters,* p. 231.
[54] *Samuel Richardson,* p. 110.
[55] fucus: a cosmetic for the skin.
[56] Bonner: Edmund Bonner (1500?-1569) who, as a much-hated Bishop of London, presided over the condemnation of various "heretics" who were later executed: hence the epithet, "bloody."
[57] Moracho: an Anglicization of the Irish surname Murchu or Murchadha; more commonly anglicized to Murphy.
[58] Scythian: The Scythians were a nomadic people living close to the Caspian sea who had been identified as barbarians by ancient Roman authors such as Tacitus. Edmund Spenser, when commenting on the state of Ireland in 1596, described several customs of the Gaelic Irish population as so close to those of the ancient Scythians that it satisfied him that they were in fact descended from the Scythians. This "proof" of the ancestry of the Gaelic Irish was accepted by other English authors to the point where Scythian became a form of derision for all Irish Catholic people.
[59] President: precedent.
[60] will: a misprint for well.
[61] Night-rail: a dressing gown.
[62] Touze: to pull someone — usually a woman — indelicately or roughly about.
[63] Chip in Porridge: a thing of little consequence; an addition (to porridge) which does no good or harm.
[64] Bravo: a daring villain, a reckless desperado.

[65] Shades: probably the quiet deserted places where the lovers had been happy together.
[66] Out-landish Man: a foreigner.
[67] Horns: the horns of the cuckold.
[68] Niobetick: from Niobe of Greek mythology who was turned to stone.
[69] Lictor: an officer whose function was to attend upon a magistrate and to execute the sentence of judgement upon offenders.
[70] Nuns: prostitutes.
[71] Bobb'd: tapped.
[72] Brachman: brahmin.
[73] Devoir: respect for.
[74] Proteus: a Greek sea-god fabled for his ability to assume various shapes; hence, one who assumes various shapes or forms.
[75] Jacobus: the name of an English gold coin struck in the reign of James I.
[76] Groat: a coin, common all over Europe, first minted in Ireland in 1460.
[77] half a Piece: a piece of money of gold or silver: cf. "thirty pieces of silver".
[78] Sarsfeild: Patrick Sarsfield fought for James II at the Battle of the Boyne, 1690, and was second-in-command in the defence of Limerick under Boisileau. Guided by the Rapparee, Galloping Hogan, he ambushed and exploded a Williamite convoy of guns and other supplies at Ballyneety, outside Limerick, August, 1690.
[79] Morion: a helmet without a visor.
[80] Teague: an anglicization of the Irish name Tadhg, hence a nickname for an Irishman.
[81] Mittimus: a warrant signed by a justice of the peace committing a person to custody, pending due process of the law.
[82] Beaver: a visor on a helmet.
[83] Rapperees: an irregular soldier of the kind which came to prominence in the years in which this work is set; a bandit or freebooter. More commonly spelled rapparee.
[84] Gust: an unusual use of the word: it appears to mean a "gust of beauty" as in a "gust of wind".
[85] Potosi: in 1546, Spanish explorers in Bolivia discovered one of the world's richest deposits of silver near Potosi.
[86] Schomberg: Friedrich Herman Duke of Schomberg (1626-1690)

was a French Huguenot career officer in the French army who left that country and took up residence in the Netherlands after the revocation of the Edict of Nantes in 1685. He accompanied William of Orange to England in 1688 when he took over the British throne from King James, and Schomberg was appointed in 1689 to command the Williamite campaign in Ireland against the Jacobite forces who had control of the country except for some outposts in Ulster. Schomberg arrived in Belfast on 12 August 1689 and took over command of the Williamite positions in Ulster and cautiously established command over most of that province. This was in preparation for an advance on Dublin which came the following year, but Schomberg was killed in the Williamite victory over the Jacobite forces at the Boyne in 1690.

[87] represented: took the place of, impersonated.